SHADOW HUNTER

Breathe . . . Joshua concentrated his entire being. *You are the void . . . you are the fire . . .*

And then he was out, beyond the ship, riding just ahead of the blast wave of his missile, barely aware of his hands moving on the control panel as the missile came up and around toward the oncoming Al'ar rocket.

Hands coming together, fingers outstretched . . .

Far away, in a safe, warm world, Wolfe's hands left the missile's control panel, splayed, then moved together. He heard Taen's hiss of alarm.

Touching . . .

Wolfe's missile veered into the path of the oncoming projectile. Flame balled over nothingness, then vanished, and a few tiny metal fragments spun down toward the rocks below.

Taen stared at Wolfe. "Shadow Warrior," he said, "now I feel fear toward you. I no longer know what you are, what you are becoming ..."

By Chris Bunch
Published by Ballantine Books:

The Shadow Warrior
THE WIND AFTER TIME
HUNT THE HEAVENS

With Allan Cole:
The Sten Adventures
STEN
THE WOLF WORLDS
THE COURT OF A THOUSAND SUNS
FLEET OF THE DAMNED
REVENGE OF THE DAMNED
THE RETURN OF THE EMPEROR
VORTEX
EMPIRE'S END

A DAUGHTER OF LIBERTY
A RECKONING FOR KINGS

THE FAR KINGDOMS
THE WARRIOR'S TALE
KINGDOMS OF THE NIGHT

Books published by The Ballantine Publishing
Group are available at quantity discounts on bulk
purchases for premium, educational, fund-raising,
and special sales use. For details, please call
1-800-733-3000.

HUNT THE HEAVENS

Book Two of *The Shadow Warrior*

Chris Bunch

A Del Rey® Book
BALLANTINE BOOKS • NEW YORK

A Del Rey® Book
Published by Ballantine Books
Copyright © 1996 by Chris Bunch

http://www.randomhouse.com

Library of Congress Catalog Card Number: 96-96322

ISBN 0-345-38736-8

Manufactured in the United States of America

First Edition: September 1996

10 9 8 7 6 5 4 3 2 1

For:

Dr. Michio Kaku,
Professor of Theoretical Physics

Master Hei Long

Grandmaster Toshitora Yamashiro,
The Nine Shadows of the Koga Ninja

* CHAPTER ONE *

The dead ships were scattered through the night, sometimes sharply illumed in white light, then darkness reclaimed its own as they moved, drifted, the rocky spray of the nearby unborn world occluding the light from the far-distant sun.

The ships were linked by nearly invisible cables that held them in an approximate orbit around a medium-size planetoid. Some of the ships were worn-out and centuries old, others were the energy-devouring military craft of the great war eleven years in the past. Some wore the colors of failed merchant enterprises, others the standards of ones too successful by far. Some appeared intact, others were being systematically cannibalized by their caretaker on the asteroid "below."

Half a light-second distant, space distorted, and there was the slight blink as a ship came out of stardrive. A few moments later, a transmission came:

"Malabar Control, Malabar Control, this is the *Grayle*. Request approach and docking instructions."

The call was made three times before a reply came in:

"*Grayle*, this is Malabar. Request your purpose. This

is not a public port. Landing permission is granted only with proper authority."

"Malabar, this is *Grayle*. Stand by." The synthed female voice was replaced by a man's:

"Malabar, this is *Grayle*. Purpose for visit: resupply."

"*Grayle*, this is Malabar. Permission refused. I say again—this is not a public port."

"Malabar, this is *Grayle*. Message follows for Cormac. I shackle Wilbur Frederick Milton unshackle. Sender: Ghost."

There was dead air, then:

"Stand by."

Nearly an hour passed before:

"*Grayle*, this is Malabar Control. Porting request granted. We have auto-approach capability. Please slave your ship controls to this frequency. After docking do not leave your ship until authorized. Cormac advises will meet Ghost personally and strongly recommends it had best be Ghost Actual. Clear."

*

The man lounging against the bulkhead wore an expensive cotton shirt faded from many washings, a sleeveless sweater that could have been his grandfather's, and khaki pants that might have belonged to a uniform once.

He straightened as the inner lock door slid open and eyed Joshua as he came out.

"Joshua," Cormac said. "If that's the name you're still using, Ghost Actual."

"It is. And you're still flying your own colors," Wolfe said.

"Time must've been good to us then."

Wolfe made no response. Cormac turned to an alcove.

"He's who he said he was, friends. You can go on about your business."

Two men carrying stubby blast rifles came out, nodded politely to Joshua, and went past into the inner reaches of the planetoid.

"Interesting how you never forget the shackle code, isn't it?" Cormac commented. "And you're right. I do owe you. What do you need? A ship? An insert, like the old days? I haven't done much direct moving lately, but I doubt if I've lost any moves. If that's what you need."

"I need a shipyard."

"Ah? You don't appear to have taken any damage, from what the screen showed me."

"I didn't. But the *Grayle*'s maybe a little too noticeable. Do you still remember how to do a Q-ship setup?"

"Do I remember?" Cormac laughed shortly. "Commander, that's one of my most requested tunes these days. There appear to be a lot of men and women floating about who'd rather not have their ships present the same face to the Federation—or to anybody—more than once or twice.

"Yes. I can handle that little job for you. How thorough a change you want? Snout, fins, configuration, signature . . . I can still do it all."

"How long for the full boat?"

"Pun intended?"

Again, Wolfe didn't answer.

Cormac considered. "Normally three months. But I assume these aren't normal times."

"You assume right," Wolfe said.

"Month and a half, then," Cormac hesitated. "That's a big call-in, I must say."

"I'll cover your costs, plus ten percent," Wolfe said. "I'm not broke. But I'd appreciate a quick turnaround."

Cormac swept a grandiose bow. "So let it be written . . . so let it be done!"

Wolfe grinned. "Where were we the last time I heard you say that?"

"I had that wonderful hollowed-out moonlet," Cormac said wistfully. "Not ten light-minutes from that Al'ar base, and they never twigged to me at all."

"What happened to it?"

"I don't know," Cormac said. "I tried to track it down when the Federation started mothballing everything." He shrugged. "I suppose someone beat me to it.

"Now wouldn't that make a *great* smuggler's haven?"

"From what I've heard about this sector," Wolfe said, "you don't appear to need one."

"True, true, too damned true. Come on. I'll show you around and start my crews to work."

"Not quite yet," Wolfe said. "I've got a passenger who nobody gets to see. I mean nobody, Cormac. How do we arrange that?"

"We'll set up quarters next to mine. No bugs, no probes, no nothing. Not even mine. You could put the Queen of Sheba there and no one would ever know."

"Good. I'll need some kind of vehicle to make the transfer."

"No problem with that, either. Now come on. Let me buy you a drink. You still drink . . . Armagnac, it was, yes?"

"You remember well."

The two men started down the long metallic corridor.

"Sometimes," Cormac said a little wistfully, "it's

about the only excitement I have. I swear I sometimes think I miss the war. You ever feel that way?"

"Not yet."

"You *are* blessed."

*

Cormac's quarters were hand-worked wood, silver, dark-red leather, lavish as a port admiral's. Wolfe lounged back against his couch, tasted his drink.

"It's only Janneau," Cormac apologized. "If I'd known you were coming I could have had one of the freetraders come up with better."

"It's fine." Wolfe looked about. "You have done well by yourself."

"It wasn't hard," Cormac said. "When peace broke out all anyone wanted was to either get out or find some nice, comfortable sinecure. Those of us who had, well, an eye for the main chance could pretty much pick and choose. And I wanted to stay out here in the Outlaw Worlds.

"I heard they needed someone to take care of all the ships that were going to be decommissioned. Given my modest talents, and a few coms to some friends who remembered what services I'd been able to render, and I had a new career, or anyway the powerbase for one."

"Doesn't the Federation ever come looking to see what's happening to those hulks?"

"Hell no. There's fifty-eight boneyards around the galaxy. Some of them don't even have caretakers, and I wonder if the ships're even still there. At least I'm disappearing mine little by little. By the way, I could make you one *hell* of a deal on a battlewagon if you're interested. One thing the Federation still has too much of, Joshua, and that's warships." Cormac picked up his glass of beer, looked at it, set it back down. "Them . . . and the people who used to pilot them."

"You do miss the war," Wolfe said gently.

"And why not? I was only twenty-two then. How many people my age had their own spaceport and responsibility for getting people into—and sometimes out of—places no sane person could imagine?"

"Why didn't you stay in? Federation Intelligence must've wanted to keep you."

"I don't have much use for some of the people they did keep," Cormac said. "I did a couple of . . . small jobs for them after the war. And was sorry I did."

"Cisco being one of them?"

"That shit-for-brains!"

"He's still with them."

"Why am I not surprised?" Cormac said. "Bastards like him have to have a big daddy to hide behind. I can remember . . . no. Leave it."

The slender man got up, walked to a bookcase, and picked up a model of a starship.

"I wasn't surprised to hear from you," he said without turning around. "Not that surprised, anyway."

"Oh?" Wolfe's tone remained casual, but one hand moved toward his waistband.

"Ghost Actual," Cormac said, "you are in a ton of trouble. Two tons."

"That's why I need the ship-change."

"You might need more than that."

Cormac went to a desk, opened it, and touched a pore-pattern lock. "This came across about an E-week ago. I pulled a copy, then iced the file. Nobody else on Malabar has seen it."

He took out a rolled cylinder of paper and handed it to Wolfe, who opened it. There was a pic on it of Wolfe that was four years old, and:

WANTED

Joshua Wolfe
for
Murder, Conspiracy,
Treason,
and
Other Crimes
Against the Federation

500,000 CREDITS REWARD
Must Be Taken Alive

"Alive, eh?" Wolfe read the rest of the sheet. "But I'm considered armed, deadly, guaranteed to resist arrest, and so forth. That ought to slow them down for a little."

"Should I ask?"

"Better not, Cormac. It gets real involved. Although I wonder how the hell they figure I've committed treason since I haven't been inside the Federation much since the war."

"It doesn't matter a tinker's fart to me," Cormac said. "Who was it who said if he had a choice between betraying his country or a friend, he hoped he'd have the balls to sell his country out?"

"Don't remember. But I don't think he said it quite like that."

"Actually," Cormac said, "I thought when I got the

call you'd be wanting . . . other changes made. Ones in-
volving a doctor."

Wolfe smiled, moved his hand away from his waist,
picked up his drink, and sipped. "I don't think I'm that
desperate yet." He set the snifter down. "Cisco's the one
who originated that warrant."

"Son of a bitch," Cormac said. "I should have slotted
him way back when. Remember when he tried to tell me
how to run a snatch-and-grab and there were about a trillion Al'ar looming down on us?"

"I do. I think that's the only time I've ever seen you
raise your voice."

"I was feeling hostile," Cormac admitted. "That man
doesn't bring out the best in me. Never mind. And forget
about paying for the ship mods."

He pushed through the beginnings of Wolfe's protests.
"That wasn't a question, goddammit. You might need the
geetus later. Hell, if you've got an open warrant, I know
you will. Sooner or later that frigging Cisco'll change the
terms and it'll be dead or alive, no questions as long as
the body bag's full. Just you wait.

"And then you'll really be sailing close to the wind.
Cisco may be a stumblebum, but he's dangerous. Especially when he's got the whole goddamned Federation for
backup."

*

Wolfe felt the walls themselves might be pulsating to
the music. The circular bar was filled, and the slide-
tempo band in the center ring was sweating hard.

Cormac leaned close. "Well?" he said, half shouting to
be heard.

"Well what?" Wolfe said.

"Well, it's been two weeks. You feel any more relaxed than when you checked in?"

Wolfe shrugged. "I'll relax when the *Grayle*'s ready to go. Lately I get twitchy when I don't have a back door."

"I'm pushing the crews as hard as I can right now. Most of the material's in-shipped. Oh, yeah—I stole a nifty piece of signature-masking electronics out of a P-boat that got dumped on me last year. Put that in today myself."

A voice said hello, and Wolfe turned. The woman was in her early twenties, had red hair in a pixie bob, and wore a designer's idea of a shipsuit, made of black velvet with see-through panels. He returned the greeting. The woman held her smile, lifted a finger, and ran it slowly over her lips, then melted into the crowd.

"You been making conquests while I'm slaving in the guts of your ship?" Cormac asked wryly.

"Hardly. Never seen her before. You know her?"

"No. I think I've seen her once. Don't even know if she's pro or just looking for action." Cormac shrugged. "You want dinner?"

Wolfe nodded, and they found a wall booth. Wolfe slid the privacy/sound one-way curtain shut and grimaced in the sudden hush. "I guess one of the drawbacks of the aging process is that music gets louder than it used to be."

"While everything else gets dimmer," Cormac agreed. "So the trick is to never get old."

The menu glimmered to life between them. Wolfe studied it, then touched the sensors for a conch salad and curried crayfish brochettes.

"You want wine?" he asked.

"Never developed a taste for it," Cormac said. "I'll stick with beer."

To accompany the meal, Wolfe ordered a half-bottle of a white whose description suggested it might resemble an Alsatian Riesling, and leaned against the back wall of the booth. Cormac touched his own sensor, and a mug of beer appeared from a trapdoor in the table's center.

"Joshua," he said carefully, "something I've wondered."

"Wonder away."

"The word was you grew up among the Al'ar. Is that right?"

"Not quite," Joshua said. "My folks were diplomats. We were on Sauros for three years. Then the Al'ar jumped the fence, and we got stuck in an internment camp." He paid deliberate attention to the drink menu and found a claimed Earth brandy. The drink arrived, Wolfe tasted it, made a face.

"Somebody's chemist needs a trip to the home planet for research. Anyway, my folks died there, and I got off, and the Federation thought I was a hot item. And the war dragged on."

"What do you think happened to the Al'ar?"

"They vanished."

"No shit! Every damned million or billion or trillion of them, zip-gone? I was out there, too, remember? Where do you think they went?"

"I don't know."

"Can they come back?"

"I . . . don't think so."

"So we had ten years and who knows how many bodies so they could pull a vanishing act. Why did they start that goddamned war, anyway?"

Joshua considered his words. "Because they wanted the same thing we do. All the room in the galaxy plus two yards. I guess space can't support but one hog at a time."

"So much for patriotism," Cormac said. "Sorry. I got the idea you aren't real fond of talking about them."

"That doesn't bother me," Wolfe said. "I don't much like talking about the war, though."

"So what do you want to talk about?"

Wolfe considered, then smiled. "What about whether that redhead was real or not?"

The trapdoor opened, and their food lifted into view. Neither man spoke as they ate. After a time Cormac looked out.

"Here she comes again. Why don't you ask her?"

"Maybe. After I finish eating."

"Looks like she's got a question of her own."

The woman came over to the booth and tapped. Wolfe found the OPEN sensor, and the music battered them.

The woman smiled and started to say something. Wolfe leaned closer.

"Joshua!" Cormac shouted, and went over the top of the table, knocking Wolfe back as a blaster beam crashed across the room and blew a hole in the booth's back wall.

Wolfe was momentarily trapped between the back of the booth and the table. Cormac rolled away and Wolfe squirmed up. The redhead's hand went into a slit in the shipsuit and flashed out with a tiny handgun.

Wolfe curled forward, smashing the table away, and his fingers snapped out and touched the woman's gunhand.

She shrieked; the gun went flying and she stumbled back as the first gunman fired again.

The blast took the woman in the back. Her body spasmed, and she flopped aside as Wolfe came out of the booth, gun in hand.

The gunman was on the other side of the band, running for the stairs that led to the upper deck.

Wolfe knelt, free hand coming up to brace the gun butt, elbow just on the far side of his knee.

Breathe . . . breathe . . . the earth holds firm . . .

His finger touched the trigger stud, and the gun bucked. The bolt took the gunman in the side, and he screamed, clawed at himself, and sagged, body slipping bonelessly down the stairs.

The room was screams and motion. Cormac was beside him, his own pistol out.

Wolfe glanced at the woman, saw dead, surprised eyes, and looked away. He went across the room, paying no attention to the hubbub, and kicked the gunman's body over.

He was young, no older than the woman his bad aim had killed, sallow-faced, with the wisp of a beginning goatee. Paying no mind to the blood pouring from the hole in the gunman's side, Wolfe quickly and expertly patted the body down.

He found no identification, but from an inner pocket took out a piece of paper that had been folded and refolded until its creases were about to wear through. He unfolded it.

Joshua Wolfe . . .

He passed the paper to Cormac, who scanned it. "Somebody missed the part about alive, alive-o," the shipyard owner said. "It appears," he went on in a near whisper, "I didn't scrub that file as clean as I thought I had. Or else word's gotten offplanet about you being here."

The room was deadly silent.

Wolfe *felt* no threat, and his gun vanished. A moment later, a woman laughed shrilly, tightly, and the volume went back up again.

"Let's go," Cormac said. "I'll fix the local heat when we're back at my grounds."

Wolfe nodded, and they moved quickly toward the exit. Wolfe opened the door for his friend, who went out and flattened against the wall. The corridor was empty.

Joshua followed him.

"I guess," he said, "maybe we *do* need to talk about some . . . further alterations."

*

Joshua Wolfe's face filled all three of the large screens. He sat in a chair in the middle of them, his expression blank.

"Are you feeling anything?"

"No."

There was a hissing, and the screens clouded as gas sprayed out around Wolfe. His face turned frosty white. After a few moments, it began swelling, turning red, as if he were being systematically hammered by invisible fists.

The other man in the white room moved away from his console and walked to Joshua's chair. He was big, imposing, and might, years earlier, before the muscle softened, have played some kind of a contact sport. He'd said he wished to be known as Brekmaker.

He walked around Joshua, stroking his chin, his eyes intent. Wolfe lay motionless in the chair, as he'd been ordered, but his eyes followed the man.

"Are you experiencing much discomfort?"

Joshua's eyes were no more than slits as the skin puffed up around them. "Not . . . that much."

"Good. In a few moments we shall proceed. This," Brekmaker went on, "is an interesting challenge. You certainly have a . . . lived-in face, my friend. Yes, I suppose that's how I'd put it." His tone suggested he wasn't used to anyone contradicting his observations.

"Now, if we had enough time, of course we could build you an entirely new face, from the bones out. Turn you into a chubby, happy-go-lucky sort. Then we could take some bone, maybe an inch or so, out of your lower legs, shorten you.

"Do some chemical alterations of your digestive system, and poof, after a few months and a thousand meals, you'd have the body to match your face. Rolo-polo, the grinning fat boy.

"I've always wanted to do a perfect job such as that," the man went on. "But I've never had the time . . . or rather my clients haven't. Nor have they properly understood my intent.

"No, they all say they want to be different, but they seldom mean it. You can talk if you want to."

Wolfe remained silent.

"So what I intend to do," Brekmaker went on, without waiting more than a moment, "is to make you into the impossible man to your friends and enemies. First we'll remove all your facial scars and marks, especially that one near your mouth. Fortunately, it's not a keloid, so removal will be quite simple.

"In the process, I'll take all of the aging lines off your neck. Then I'm going to build up your cheekbones a bit, make them a bit more distinct than they already are. I'm going to rebuild that nose, which looks like it's been broken more than once, am I right?"

"Three, maybe four times," Wolfe mumbled.

"In short, I'm going to be your Ponce de Léon. In case you don't know—"

"I know who he was," Wolfe said.

"Oh. Not many of my clients have heard about the Fountain of Youth. Yes, you'll be the young man you once were, plus I'll make some improvements the helix didn't give you when you were born. I'll also take some of the pouching off your eyelids, cut a bit of cartilage from the back of your ears and pin them back a little just because they're a bit too batlike for my tastes.

"You haven't had significant hair loss, so I won't need to do implants, but I will do a perma-dark so you won't be a silver fox anymore.

"Of course, you're wondering right now how all this is going to make you unrecognizable to . . . to whoever you don't wish to know you.

"It's very simple but devilishly clever, if I do say so myself. Imagine this, Mister, uh, Taylor you said your name was, I believe. Imagine you are walking down the street and you see someone who you recognize from your first time in prison, or in school, or whatever, twenty years ago. He looks *exactly* the same as he did then. You are about to hail him and then you stop yourself, barely in time.

"You're embarrassed, because you realize that all of us change in ten or fifteen or twenty years, and of course anyone who looked exactly like your friend of years ago cannot, simply cannot, be that man.

"And so you hurry past, not really looking at this person again, because you're deeply grateful you didn't say anything and make an utter ass of yourself and also don't think on the matter, for none of us wish to remember our momentary near foolishnesses.

"Simple . . . yet very clever, isn't it?"

Wolfe managed to make a noise that might have been agreement.

"I feel that you're experiencing a bit of pain." Brekmaker went to his control panel, touched sensors. Gas hissed. "There. That should take it away. Now we can begin."

His fingers moved over other parts of the panel, and, from the ceiling, tiny projectors appeared and moved toward Joshua's face.

*

"Culan in a kennel," Cormac swore. "You look like ratshit on rye! What'd you look like yesterday when the quack got through? Couldn't have been worse."

"Don't be so polite," Wolfe said muffledly. He glanced in the mirror beside his bed, saw the yellow-serum-crusted mask that looked like an inflated balloon, then pointedly turned the mirror facedown. "Just think of me as about to begin my butterfly imitation."

"You need anything? You sure that bastard didn't work you over with a bat or something?"

"It feels like he did."

"You need more painkiller?"

"No. I'll handle it."

"What can I get you?"

"Nothing. Just make sure Brekmaker doesn't get off-world before this whole thing's over with. I'm not real comfortable with having to pay him up front."

"Don't worry about that. I disabled the drive on his ship, and I've got one of my boys watching him pretty close. But I don't think we've got any worries, since we've got his pretty little portable OR set up in here and out of his ship. I'm sure he won't skip without it.

"He wanted to circulate, but I told him he couldn't. Not until you said it was okay.

"So he asked if I could set him up with a woman or two. The bastard likes to brag on himself. Couldn't wait to tell the girls I sent him how great a surgeon he'd been and still was even if he'd been subjected to some terrible misunderstandings, how he'd done work on Earth itself, sometimes on some of the most famous people, and so on and so forth."

"That doesn't sound like someone we want wandering around with his mouth at full drive," Wolfe said.

"I suggested just that quite strongly, and he pissed and moaned, and eventually said it'd add another ten thou to his bill."

"I'll pay it," Wolfe said.

"I wish I'd been able to get somebody else," Cormac said. "But you were in a hurry."

"What're the odds any other disbarred doc'd be different? At least he doesn't have a jar in his nose or an injector in his arm."

"So far," Cormac said glumly. "Look, I've got to get back to it. If I bust ass, about the time you start looking like a human being, I might have something to show you. You sure you don't need anything?"

"I'm sure."

Cormac left the apartment. Wolfe heard the outer door close, then lock. There was no sound but the soft murmur of music from the player in the apartment's central room and the hiss of the air recycler.

Then he *felt* the presence.

"May I enter your burrow?"

"You may."

There was a long silence. Then the other said, still in the same language:

"How unusual. Using the same senses you have, I see there shall be a vast difference. But beyond, you remain as you were. I am curious to see, once you are healed, what your own seeing shall grant you. I must say, you are incredibly ugly at the moment, even more so than normal to me."

"I'm not trying to fool *you*," Wolfe said, changing languages. "Just all these goddamned people who want my ass on toast for wanting to help you."

The other also changed to Terran. "I listened to what that Cormac said and assume he meant the ship will be ready.

"I have been wondering something. I sought the Mother Lumina, even though I have, as yet, no concrete proof of its existence. Was I correct in that? Or should I have been searching for the handful of other Al'ar whom I must believe were left behind when my people made The Crossing? I bow to your wisdom in this."

"The Mother Lumina, or your Guardians?" Wolfe said. "You seemed most convinced of the Guardians' existence when you first explained your search."

"I was and am."

"I don't know," Wolfe said.

He reached in the table beside his bed, took out the Lumina he'd taken from the cache of a thief he'd killed, touched it.

The gray stone came to life, and a thousand colors pulsed through the room, flickering over Wolfe's ruined face.

*

Joshua came suddenly awake.

"You shouted," said the one beside him. **"Are you experiencing pain?"**

"No," Joshua said. "At least . . . not much. No. I was in a dream. No, not a dream. I was being attacked. By . . . I do not know what. I heard a buzzing, though. Such as insects make."

"There are no insects on this artificial world," the other said. "Or there should not be, at any rate. So of course it must have been a dream."

"I know."

"Look at your arm," his companion said suddenly.

Wolfe's forearm showed red ridges, streaks.

"What could that be?"

"I don't know. Maybe a reaction to the painkiller?"

"But you have taken none since this afternoon."

"I don't know." Wolfe stared at the marks. Slowly they began to fade.

Then he heard, in his mind, the sound of angry insects once more.

*

"Actually, I would like to have some trumpets for a proper fanfare," Brekmaker said. "You have been an excellent subject. Now, take a look at yourself."

Joshua looked at the three screens.

"I look like me," he said. "Quite awhile ago. And I'm bright pink."

"That'll change. I'm going to put you out again, and repigment the skin. One thing, Mister Taylor. I must caution you to work on your facial reflexes. If you frown as you always frowned, if you smile as you always smiled, then the lines will start coming back, and your resemblance to your former self will become far more marked than otherwise.

"Now, lie back. You'll be unconscious for perhaps half an hour or an hour while I finish up this last detail. I'll revive you, then we can begin arrangements to reload my apparatus, and, well, the remainder of my fee, which I discussed with your associate."

"I'd just as soon stay conscious."

"No, you wouldn't. Even though repigmentation is simple, it can be quite painful. Trust me on this."

Wolfe stared at Brekmaker, grudged a nod.

"Now, I'm going to give you the deep tan of a man who's been in space, as you wished. Please put your head back on the rest."

Wolfe obeyed. The doctor fingered controls; two projectors rose out of the chair, aimed at Joshua, and anesthetic gas hissed.

"Breathe deeply now."

A few seconds later, Wolfe went limp.

The doctor used other controls, and the projectors disappeared and other, similar devices emerged. Brekmaker moved slide pots, then fingered a sensor. He watched the screens closely as a thin mist came out, his fingers dancing across a keyboard. The sprayers moved obediently, and Joshua's face darkened, changed.

"There," Brekmaker said to himself. He got out of his chair, smiling oddly.

He reached under his console and took out a small tri-di recorder. He snapped an experimental picture, then went to Joshua.

Aiming carefully, he shot a series of pictures from several angles, whistling through his teeth. He frowned, then lifted the recorder for a final shot.

There was a slight sound behind him.

Brekmaker spun, one hand diving into the pocket of his surgical gown. He saw an open panel that he thought had been bare wall.

Nearly on him was a tall, impossibly slender snake-headed being, its skin color the dead white of a drowned man. Its eyes were slitted above the hood that flared around its neck.

Brekmaker's hand came out with his gun, and his mouth opened, to shout, to scream. But as the gun lifted, the Al'ar's grasping organ flashed out, touched the doctor in midchest.

The man's face purpled. His frozen muscles tried to pull in air, failed. The gun fell limply to the deck.

Brekmaker clawed at his throat and once more the alien struck, a bare touch against the man's forehead.

Brekmaker stumbled forward, crashed across his

control console, and rolled to the floor, lying faceup, his final expression one of utter disbelief.

The Al'ar looked once at the corpse, then fitted himself awkwardly into the doctor's chair and began to wait.

* CHAPTER TWO *

"Blackmail?"

"Sure," Wolfe said. "You wait till you're at a good safe distance, then let your patient know you just happen to have taken some before-and-after pics for your professional files, and certainly the poor sod would be happy to kick in a few credits to make sure those pics are kept properly secure. It ain't a new racket."

"I'm not doing too good on the professional recommendation circuit, am I?" Cormac said. He opened up the tiny recorder, took out its microfiche, and snapped it four times in his fingers, paying close attention to what he was doing. Without looking up, in a deliberately casual voice, he asked, "Brekmaker was fool enough to take these snaps when you were conscious *and* gave you room enough to take him?"

Wolfe made no reply. Cormac looked at him, then away.

"Civilian life's getting to you," Joshua said. "You never used to ask any questions about anything."

Cormac smiled, a bit ruefully. "Sorry. Didn't mean to be inquisitive."

"Forget it."

*

The Al'ar evaded the blow, knelt, and his leg snapped out. The kick took Joshua in the upper thigh, and he hissed pain, rolled backward, then to the side as the Al'ar leapt toward him.

The Al'ar struck, Joshua sidestepped, blocked, and his return blow was blocked in return.

The two broke contact.

The Lumina stone on the pedestal against the wall of the bare room flared colors, and the Al'ar shimmered, vanished.

Wolfe glanced at the Lumina, sweat beading his forehead. The stone turned to dull gray, and the Al'ar was visible once more, closing on Wolfe.

Joshua jump-kicked, took the Al'ar in the chest, and knocked him flat. The alien backrolled into a crouch, and two fingers of Joshua's right hand hovered motionless an inch in front of his eyes.

The Al'ar froze and his hood flared. He lifted his grasping organs, crossed them.

"You have the advantage."

Wolfe bowed, stepped back, and the Al'ar got up.

"That trick with the Lumina. I did not know you could do that," the alien said.

"I did not, either. This was the first time."

"Shadow Warrior, perhaps it is good that we are searching together. Perhaps, when ... if we find the Mother Lumina, you might then be more able to understand its purpose than I.

"I might even wonder if this is what the one we went to intended, so long ago, who listened to the words you spoke and gave you your name. Perhaps

he was also one of those who remained behind and we may ask if ... when ... we meet him. But that is for the future. As I said, perhaps that Guardian sensed that you might be a more worthy user of our devices than even an Al'ar."

"You grant high praise, Taen." Wolfe switched to Terran. "Shall we go one more turn?"

"I think not. I feel fatigued."

"You're getting old, my friend."

"As are we all. In my case, perhaps it is being forced to live on Terran food. My body is not content. Last night, when my body was in disuse, I had thoughts come that were disturbing."

"You *were* corrupted by being around me. I thought Al'ar never dream."

"Not in your terms. Let me go on. I *felt* that insectlike buzzing you described. With it came a sense of dread, of menace. Then I returned my body to its proper state of readiness, and the sound was gone. Of course, I showed none of the physical signs you evinced."

"So what does it mean?"

"I do not know. But I think we must accept that this sending, or whatever it should be called, is not a fiction, but something that exists in or close to our space-time."

*

Static hummed, clicked, and SIGNAL INTERRUPT bleeped, then the screen showed CONTACT RESTORED.

"Sorry," Joshua said. "Thought I lost you for a second."

"You're still not giving me a picture," the distorted voice light-years distant complained.

"No. Nor are you."

The speaker transmitted a sound that might have been

laughter. "Isn't it nice to find a couple of professionals who really trust each other?"

"Just like always," Wolfe agreed.

"So what can I do you out of?"

"I just wanted to touch base. See if anything . . . interesting's going on."

There was dead air for almost a minute. "How clean is your transmission?"

"Clean. It's bounced, well, let's just say more than twice. And it's as sealed as I could make it."

"Okay. Only because I like to see things stirred up. Cisco's looking for you. Looking hard."

"That's no news. He's got a warrant out on me," Wolfe said.

"That's one thing," the voice said. "That's the official policy. He's put word out that he wants a meet with you. Your terms, your ground, you know how to contact him."

"Yeah. Sure. So he can collect the bounty?"

"Come on, Wolfe. Stop playing games. You know the rules."

"I'm not sure Cisco does anymore."

"No skin off my ass either way. I'm just passing the word along. There's one other thing that goes with it—he said you can bring your friend from Tworn Station along."

Wolfe waited until he could control his voice. Tworn Station was the undersea resort where he'd tracked down Taen.

"I got what you said . . . but don't know what it means."

The speaker stayed silent.

"Anything else?"

"Nope," the voice said. "Unless you want the hot gossip on who's sleeping with whom or who backalleyed her latest best friend. One other thing. Shoa InterGee is looking to hire a hotrod to take over their security section. The pay's good, but I gotta warn you, their system stinks. I've been known to go wading in their stuff every now and then for giggles, and there's folks out there far sneakier'n I am."

"Hardly think they'd be interested in hiring somebody who's on the run from FI."

"As I said, I'm just the pipeline."

"Thanks. Stay clean and I'll catch you next shout." Wolfe touched the sensor, and the speaker went dead. He turned to Taen.

"I understood the transmission," the Al'ar said in Terran. "So this Cisco knows I exist and that we are teamed. I am hardly surprised—there were more than enough people who saw me when we retreated from my ship for Federation Intelligence to draw the correct assessment.

"But it will undoubtedly make life more interesting. My question is, should we agree to this meeting with the Intelligence man?"

Wolfe considered.

"The problem," he mused aloud, "is how to walk into his nest and be able to get back out again. Mmmh. I think I can manage that."

"I was hoping you would say that. I would appreciate any data we can absorb. We are operating with far too little input in our quest," Taen said. "Now, once we derive whatever information we are able, can we kill this Cisco?"

Wolfe grinned. "Taen, you would have made a perfectly wonderful spy, what with your sense of morality and all."

"Your words are meaningless. If you have an enemy, you seek him out and slay him. All else is nothing but noise to my brain."

*

The door to Cormac's inner office opened, and a soberly dressed man with a neat beard came out. He looked at Joshua, said "Good morning, son," then went out the door, letting the door ease shut against his hand.

Wolfe looked thoughtful, shut off the com he'd been scanning, and went into Cormac's office.

"The gentleman who just left called me son. I don't think he actually had five years on me."

"Better get used to it, young man. I've already put the word out for my bars to start making sure you're of proper drinking age. Ain't surgery wonderful? Drag up a chair."

Wolfe obeyed. "Can I be nosy?"

"You cut my fingers off when *I* tried, but go ahead."

"That gentleman who just left? Was he a Chitet?"

"He certainly was, although he didn't sound like one for a couple of moments after I turned him down. He got a little dramatic on me. You have an interest in their little operation?"

"I do. They've tried to kill me half a dozen times now."

"Mercy Maude," Cormac said. "All this from an organization that claims to be nothing more than a logical and systematic philosophy and way of life.

"Then you'll be very amused when you find out what

he wanted. He put it most subtly, but he was very interested in acquiring, for a very impressive price, in cash to be handed to me directly, some of the mothballed Federation ships I'm supposed to be keeping all safe and secure. I don't mind selling a part here or there, but his ideas seemed excessive."

"They're on the move, Cormac," Wolfe said. "The last time they tried to slot me was with an *Ashida*-class cruiser."

"Oh? Not the most subtle way to suggest they don't like the way you cut your hair. And here my fine-feathered friend was telling me how they really needed half a dozen big ships to convert into transports for a large shipping deal they're about to sign. He was real specific about what he wanted: those three *Nelson*-class battleships, two of the heavy cruisers I've got, and by the way, there's a C & C rig out there that'd be almost perfect. Looks to me, if they need Command and Control, they're building a fleet. Got a bit hostile when I told him to pack his ass with salt and piddle up a rope. Most civilly and in my most mellifluous tones, of course."

"Why'd you turn them down?"

"To be honest?"

Wolfe grinned. "If that's the best option you can come up with."

"I couldn't figure out what story I'd have if somebody ever came looking for them and asked me to explain a hole in space. Although now I'm getting a little concerned for some of my confreres who don't have the well-developed sense of survival I do. As I said before, there's a lot of available warships out here in the Outlaw Worlds.

"You know, Joshua, people with a goddamned mission in life who know what I should be doing better than I do make me nervous. Especially when they start buying guns."

"You and me both," Wolfe agreed. "A small suggestion—keep your back against a wall for the next few forevers. These Chitet don't seem to handle rejection well."

"So I gather. Fortunately, my cowardice genes are well developed."

Cormac got up from his desk. " 'Tis a parlous world," he said. "I guess the only option for honest folk like you and me is to have a drink. C'mon."

*

"What were you looking for when the FI robot got pictures of you on Sauros and put me in motion?" Wolfe asked.

"I had landed on several of our homeworlds already, looking for any data that might give me a clue to the Mother Lumina," Taen said. "I hoped to consult certain files, I think your word is, from our Farseeing Division, what you call Intelligence."

"Hasn't FI already seized those?"

"They think they have," the Al'ar said. "But there are other copies, available for those who know where to look."

"What data did you specifically seek?"

"What I sought, I never found. Mention of the Mother Lumina, mention of the Guardians, anything that might have been transmitted before my people made The Crossing."

"And?"

"Nothing."

"I cannot believe," Wolfe said, "that at one signal, a signal you say you didn't receive, every frigging Al'ar in the galaxy went away like a Boojum. So you weren't looking in the right place, or in the right manner."

"I dislike your levity, but I must concede, logically, you are correct."

"Which of the homeworlds, what we call the capital worlds, were the most important?"

"Sauros," Taen said. "The world I had my birth-burrow on, the same one you lived on before the war. I also sought access to one of our great machine-thinkers, computers, to help me analyze the problem. But I had no time to search for anything before that spy-probe found me."

"If I can put us both back on Sauros, will you let me help in the search?"

The Al'ar curled on a ladder that was the closest approximation Wolfe could find to his customary seat. He remained silent for a long time. Twice his hood puffed, deflated.

"There are risks," he said. "To us both. There will be precautions still in place, unless they were set off by Federation searchers earlier. And I do not believe the Federation even knew where to look."

"I've seen Al'ar booby traps," Joshua said. "They can be managed."

"So you have a plan?"

"An idea."

"Which of my two goals are we seeking?"

"Not the Mother Lumina. We'll start with The Guardians. Maybe that'll lead us to the rock in question."

Taen's slitted eyes stared at Wolfe. "One thing you

have never told me. Not honestly, by what I can feel of your thoughts. You could have abandoned me on Montana Keep, or simply returned me to one of my own worlds, and then gone to ground.

"I do not doubt you have more than enough abilities to avoid both the Chitet and Federation Intelligence. They will not seek you forever, especially when they learn you have taken no further interest in the fate of the Al'ar.

"Why, Joshua Wolfe? Why, One Who Fights From Shadows?"

There was a long, heavy silence.

Wolfe shook his head slowly from side to side.

*

"She sings, she dances, she sways, she swoops," Cormac said proudly. He and Wolfe stood on a cross-walk in an enormous bay. Below them lay Wolfe's ship. It looked just as it had when he ported at Malabar. "Would you care to request your good ship *Lollypop* to go through her paces?"

He handed a transponder to Joshua.

"Do you hear me?" Joshua asked the ship.

"I hear you," came through the small speaker. *"I recognize your voice. Do you have a command for me?"*

Joshua turned to Cormac. "So what do I ask for?"

"How about 'gimme the external dimensions of a *Hatteras*-type 92 yacht?' In case you forget your *Jane's*, that's about twenty feet longer than the *Grayle* and a whole lot humpier."

Joshua spoke into the transponder.

"Understood," his ship said.

He heard the hiss of hydraulics, and the *Grayle* grew

imperceptibly. As she did, a long oval atop her hull lifted, and a portholed bridge appeared.

"That's all false front, of course," Cormac said. "It extends back over the drive tubes, so you don't really pick up twenty feet, and the bridge is a dummy, too. I couldn't figure any way to mickey up hull blisters, either, that wouldn't conflict with your retractable ones, so I left that alone.

"The *Grayle* can physically mimic about twenty other ships more or less of her class, from a *Foss*-class tug, to any number of in-system workships, to one of the new Federation *Sorge*-type spyships. That might be an interesting switch if things get sticky with our friend Cisco.

"But that's the frosting on the iceberg, when somebody gets too close. The real changes are in the various signatures, infrared, radar, and so forth. Onscreen, your little putt-putt can look like almost anything from a medium cruiser down to a miner's asteroid puddle jumper. That's the real prize. I decided that everybody wants to go small when they're phonying up what their ship looks like, so I'd go mostly the other way around.

"Plus your rig's pretty clean anyway, so I wouldn't be able to get much tinier an echo.

"You lost two storerooms and one of your spare staterooms for all the e-junk I loaded in, and you don't even want to think about drive economy, especially if you're using any of the drive-signature spoofers.

"Your performance envelope is still the same, unless you're using any of the physical phonies in-atmosphere. I went for things that had lots of little bitty stickouts, so there's a lot more drag. Be a little cautious about going full tilt when you're surrounded by air if you've got any of that crap extruded. I don't guarantee my welds that far."

"You through?"

"I think so."

"Pretty good spiel," Wolfe said.

"Pretty good *work*," Cormac replied. "Now you owe me."

"I do that."

Cormac turned serious. "And that's a favor I'm going to call in."

*

Wolfe was almost asleep, nodding over a last Armagnac and *Murder in the Cathedral* when the buzzing grew in his ears. He came fully awake, but the sound didn't stop; it grew still louder.

He felt menace, danger, and in spite of himself looked around the familiar bridge.

Pain seared his arm, and he pulled his sleeve back and saw the red welts emerge.

Then the buzzing was gone, and there was utter silence.

After a time, the welts subsided.

Wolfe got up, made strong coffee.

*

"De Montel?" Wolfe whistled. "This is a *serious* favor."

Cormac ran a thumbnail through the foil and pulled the cork. "Now that's what a proper bottle-opening ought to sound like," he said. "Never could get used to that crack when the pressure seal breaks."

There were two snifters on his desk. He poured one about half full, about an inch into the other.

"Thought you didn't touch hard stuff," Wolfe said.

"I'm trying to be sociable."

Wolfe sniffed, tasted, nodded. He eased himself down into the armchair in front of the desk. "Okay. What've you got?"

Cormac reached into his desk drawer, took out a holo, passed it to Joshua. "Remember her?"

The woman in the holo had dark, curly hair that frothed down about the shoulders of the sea-green gown she wore. She was on a promenade deck of a ship, and behind her a planet's curve arced. She'd evidently been told to look happy for the recorder and was trying her best to comply, without much success.

Wolfe blanked the background and the jewels at her throat, and studied her face. "I think so. From the war?"

Cormac nodded.

"Little bitty thing? A first looey . . . no. Captain."

"That's her. She was my log officer. Rita Sidamo."

"Okay. I've got her. What's her problem?"

"She's married to a shithead who won't let her leave."

Wolfe lifted an eyebrow. "No offense. But that's a little thin these days. It's too easy to just walk out . . . or scream for help."

Cormac didn't respond to that, but went on. "We were, well, pretty friendly for three or four months before the war ended. Against regs, naturally, but who gave a damn? It was pretty intense, actually.

"Since the war ended so quickly, it kind of left us hanging. We weren't sure whether we wanted to stay together, or what.

"She took her discharge, went back to her homeworld inside the Federation. We sent a few coms back and forth, and then all of a sudden she stopped writing."

Cormac picked up his drink, tasted it, and grimaced. He went to the cooler and came back with a beer.

"I got over it. Or thought I did, anyway. What the hell, we all kid ourselves about things.

"Three months ago, I got that pic and a letter. She said she had to pay someone to get it out for her."

"Out of where?"

"The reason she stopped writing is that she got married. Real quick, for no good reason, she said. I guess it was because the guy was good-looking and rich."

"This isn't sounding any thicker, Cormac."

Cormac's lips tightened. He opened his desk again, took out a microfiche, stuck it into the viewer on the desk, and spun the device until the plate was facing Wolfe.

An image was onscreen:

A man about Joshua's size, dark-haired, harsh features, staring into the recorder lens with a challenging look.

"His name is Jalon Kakara. He's a merchant fleet owner. Has his own shipyard."

Other images, starting with a tab's screamer:

BEHIND THE MASK: JALON KAKARA'S PRIVATE SINWORLD

"He's got his own planetoid, which he calls Nepenthe. It's inside the Federation," Cormac said. "I don't know about the sin part of it. But it looks pretty spectacular."

Wolfe nodded absently, watching images flash past: a long spaceyacht; two mansions; a gleaming high office building; a domed, irregularly shaped planetoid; a spaceport with its pads about half full, all of the ships with jagged crimson streaks down their sides; laughing, richly dressed people at some sort of party; then a picture of Kakara and the woman, both wearing swimsuits, sitting on the rail of an antique hovercraft.

"He's a shit," Cormac said flatly.

"I've never heard of the guy," Wolfe said. "But that doesn't mean anything. The pics make him look rich, all right. Sorry I said what I did."

He drank and Cormac refilled the snifter.

"I've done some research. Had some friends inside the Federation get what they could on him. Kakara does most of his business from Nepenthe," Cormac said. "When he goes offworld, he has his own yacht. Actually, it's a full-size *Desdemona*-type freighter he had laid down in his yards and modified to his specs.

"Sometimes he lets Rita go along with him. But mostly, she's stuck on Nepenthe. Especially now."

"I've known people who'd like to be stuck like that."

"His biggest thrill is getting in the pants of his friends' women," Cormac said. "And he's a hitter."

Wolfe's face tightened.

"She wanted out, told him so, even managed to file divorce papers. He got to the records and blanked them. Told her she's his, she agreed, and that settled things. Period.

"She said he likes it better now that she's a prisoner."

"Are you asking me to do something about it?"

"No," Cormac said. "I wouldn't do that. But I'd like you to come up with a plan for me."

"For *you*? Cormac, you're a goddamned driver, not an op. You're the guy who gets people like me in and out, remember?"

Cormac stared at Wolfe. "Eleven years since I've seen

her. And even before I got the letter I kept thinking about her, and feeling like a dickhead because I should've gone after her way back then, done something, but I didn't. So this time I'm going to.

"I'd already made up my mind before you showed up. When you did ... I figured maybe I actually had a chance."

Wolfe took a deep breath. "Are there kids?"

"No. She said that was one reason things went wrong."

"Do you have a way of contacting her?"

"No."

"So you want me to come up with a way for you to get your butt down on Nepenthe, get to her, tell her your idea, hope to Hades she wasn't having a momentary fit of pique at the old man, and then haul ass out with your lovely like you're a harpless Orpheus, right?"

Cormac nodded.

"You realize you're going to get killed pulling this stupid piece of knightly virtue, don't you?"

Cormac shrugged.

Wolfe picked up the glass of Armagnac and drained it.

*

"You are not going to like this," Wolfe said to Taen. "I'm not sure I do myself. But circumstances have altered our plans."

* CHAPTER THREE *

"This was a decision reached without logical consideration," the Al'ar said. His neck hood was half flared.

"No question about that," Wolfe agreed.

"I have more input on our dreams of insects," Taen said. "I sense blue, I sense hazard, a danger that reaches beyond me, beyond you. That should be our immediate concern, not this person who may or may not desire to mate with your friend."

"Your data," Wolfe said dryly, still in Terran, "was derived from cold, logical analysis."

"Certainly," Taen said. "My brain has no other capabilities."

"But what my brain does is . . . never mind."

Taen's hood slowly subsided. He stared long at Wolfe.

"Do you remember our first meeting?" he said, returning to Al'ar. "You were being tested by some Al'ar hatchlings until my presence interceded."

"We'll forget that I had just busted one clown's ribs for being so interested in tests. Go ahead."

"You called them cowards at the time, which there is no word for in Al'ar, because they had the sense to

39

attack you in a group rather than singly. I did not understand the term then and am not sure I understand it now.

"But let me tell you of another occurrence I witnessed. During the war, after my special unit was dissolved and I'd been ordered to abandon my hunt for you, I was on the command deck of one of our ships, the kind we called a Large Ship Killer. We trapped two Federation probes and disabled one's drive unit with a long-lance striker. The second ship would have been able to escape, most likely, while we delayed to destroy the first.

"Instead, it reset its pattern and came back almost certainly in an attempt to rescue those who were aboard the first, which any rational analysis would have determined was futile, since they were doomed. The result was we destroyed both ships and their crews."

"Humans do stupid things like that," Wolfe said.

"Is the thought process, or rather emotional pattern, because there is no way it can be of rational derivation, which occurred to the captain of that second ship similar in any way to why you wish to aid Cormac?"

"Possibly."

"Could this sort of thinking, which no Al'ar could ever comprehend, have anything to do with the fact you were defeating my people before we chose to avoid destruction and make The Crossing?"

"Probably not," Wolfe said. "We were just lucky." He got up from his chair. "Come on, little horse. We have miles to go before we sleep."

"I doubt if I shall ever understand."

"That makes two of us."

*

Wolfe knelt in front of the Lumina, naked, his hands on his knees. The stone flared colors around the padded room. His breathing was slow, deep.

I am in the void . . . I am the void . . . there is nothing beyond, there is nothing before . . .

He lifted his hands, brought palms together, clasped them, forefinger extended.

Fire, burn, fire enter, fill, bring wisdom . . .

His breathing slowed still further.

Quite suddenly, he was "above" the Lumina, "looking" down at it. He moved still higher, reached the overhead, passed through it, mind giving a "picture" of conduits, bare, oiled steel, then he was "on" the control deck.

His breathing quickened, and he was staring at the Lumina as its colors flamed. He turned his head and unclasped his hands; the stone cooled, turned gray.

"Well, I shall be dipped," he said in considerable astonishment. "I didn't know—"

He broke off, centered his mind, brought control over his breathing. Once more, it slowed.

The Lumina came "alive," colors seething.

Wolfe saw nothing but the stone, nor did his perception change.

After long moments, he stood, without using his hands. The Lumina's colors subsided.

Joshua shook his head in bewilderment, picked up the Lumina, and went toward the fresher.

*

"In readiness for last jump before arrival off Garrapata," the ship said.

"Stand by," Wolfe said. He scanned the screen once more. "And now we go into the Federation itself and wiggle our butts.

"Let's see how well it works in the real world. We want a physical transformation here, not just a spoof-job. Assume the characteristics of . . . a converted *YS*-class yardboat. I bought you after the war, did most of the conversion myself. I renamed you the, umm, *Otranto*. Respond to any calls to that designation as well as *Grayle* until ordered otherwise."

"Understood. Stand by."

Hydraulics hummed, and indicators on a newly installed control panel moved.

"Conversion complete," the ship said.

"Now how the hell can I take a look at . . . extrude damage-inspection recorder fifty yards, give full angle of yourself."

"Understood."

After a few moments, a screen opened.

"Damn," Wolfe said in some amazement. "I'd hardly recognize you myself. I'd say you were gorgeous, except that from your appearance I'm a pretty hamfisted makeup artist if I did the work myself. I better put a beeper on you when we land so I don't get lost."

"Your friend Cormac," Taen said, "did excellent work. He is to be commended. It appears that your ship will serve us well."

"He's getting his paybacks. Ship, what do you think? I remember your last programmer decided you needed more of a personality."

"Your statements I interpreted as showing pleasure. Therefore, I feel the same, although I know not what the term means."

"*Grayle*, meet Taen. You'd make a great pair. We'll resurrect ENIAC to perform the ceremony. Okay, *Otranto*. Jump when you're ready."

The world shifted, turned, and Joshua tasted strange spices, felt memories come to him. Then all was normal, and the screens showed new constellations.

"N-space exited," the ship reported. *"Garrapata two E-days distant."*

*

The office, and the little man sitting in it, smelled of failure that'd hung on so long it'd become his best friend.

"Here," he said. "It's quite a package. Well worth the price I named, Mister . . . Taylor." The man's nose twitched above his sparse mustache. He reminded Wolfe of a rabbit about to enter a carrot patch.

Wolfe took the microfiche, hefted it, *felt* it. "Who made the stonebucket?"

The little man tried anger, found it unfamiliar, gave it up. "You don't think I did it?"

"I know you didn't. Not enough time, for openers. But I don't give a damn."

"Okay," the man said. "It was put together by a team from DeGrasse, Hathaway. I have a way in with somebody who contracts for them now and again. I didn't figure there was much cause for doubling the work they did. I've never heard anybody complain about their investigations." The little man hesitated, then went on. "Plus Kakara's little planet isn't that far away, and he does a lot of business here on Garrapata. He's got a reputation. It's hard to watch your back when there's only one of you."

"Who were DeGrasse, Hathaway digging for?"

"Don't know. Wouldn't ask."

Wolfe put the fiche inside his jacket, took out bills. "Here's your fee. You said you preferred cash."

"Who doesn't?"

Wolfe left the tiny office, eased the door shut. Its click was the loudest sound in the dusty corridor.

*

Joshua stepped out of the shuttle, walked unhurriedly to a nearby dock, slipped around it, waited. No one was following after him.

He crossed back, past the shuttle station to a second dock, got into the smaller, personnel elevator, and touched its sensor. The lift went up to the deck of the oval dock. He touched the pore-sensor on the *Grayle*'s lock, entered.

Taen sat curled in the stand the two had welded together a day earlier in the *Grayle*'s tiny machine shop. A heavy blaster lay beside him, on its shelf. His eyes slid open.

"There is a message," he said with no further greeting.

Wolfe went up the spiral staircase to the command deck and to the com.

The screen blurred as he played back. He saw Cisco's utterly unmemorable face.

"I received your blurt-signal," the Intelligence executive said. "I assume you have our mutual friend. I need to meet you. It'll do you more good than me. The situation has altered since we last spoke as regards him . . . and yourself.

"We'll meet on your terms, your turf. Contact me as to

details through any of the usual channels. I guarantee your safety, but I know you don't believe me."

"You're right," Joshua said to the fading image. "I don't."

*

Jalon Kakara glowered at Wolfe. Joshua got up and walked around the holo, examining it closely.

"Did you notice," Taen said in Terran, "how his eyes never quite looked into the pickup?"

"I'll be damned. No."

"Not in this image, nor in any of the others."

"If I believed baddies had consciences, which I don't, I'd suspect Jalon has trouble sleeping nights." Wolfe went back to the controls, continued scrolling the microfiche.

"I have a thought," the Al'ar said. "By the way. I think I should speak in Terran until we return to the Outlaw Worlds. Sound can sometimes travel much farther and arouse greater suspicion than what we see.

"I am sorry. I am interrupting your concentration."

"No, you're not," Wolfe said. "I'm just cycling this and letting my subconscious do the scheming. Go ahead."

"My idea was that perhaps I was wrong."

"An Al'ar admitting he was wrong? You *were* corrupted by me, and I understand why your people abandoned you."

"I define that as a joke and pay it no mind, nor will I allow the insult to require a response. Perhaps, in a way, we shall benefit from this idiotic side-turning away from our proper goals."

"In what way?"

"Very few Al'ar ever left their own worlds and jour-
neyed into the Federation. Possibly this is yet another
reason we lost the war, since ignorance is always a
weapon that turns in your hand.

"I shall pay close attention to what transpires, since I
know we will not manage to reach our goals without in-
terference from the Federation. I must know my enemy
better than any Al'ar ever did."

"Your enemy . . . and mine," Wolfe said, suddenly grim.

He touched sensors, and once more Jalon Kakara's
eyes filled with casual disdain and enmity.

"No," he murmured, and touched more buttons.

The alien and the man were suddenly in the middle of
a party, Kakara the center of attention. Wolfe glanced
again at the woman beside him, recognized her as Rita
Sidamo, but only with a part of his mind.

His eyes were held by the inaudible conversation
Kakara was having with a waiter. The man's face was
nearly as white as his antique boiled shirt. Suddenly
Kakara's hand shot out, sent the servant's tray spinning.

Kakara was shouting now, and the smaller man began
trembling.

Taen began to ask something, stopped when Wolfe
motioned for silence. He ran the scene once more, then
again.

"Oh, I like a bully," he said softly. "Especially on
toast."

*

The bar was a quiet hush, its liquor almost as old as the
money it served. It even had human bartenders.

Joshua Wolfe eased into a seat not far distant from one
bartender, whose dignified face suggested he would be

more suited on the other side of the long polished wooden slab.

"Your wish, sir?"

"Armagnac, if you have it."

"We do. Any special label?"

"I'm impressed," Wolfe said. "Rare enough to find any Armagnac. I'll have Hubert Dayton."

"I am sorry, sir. But I doubt if you could find that anywhere but Earth. Possibly not even outside of Bas-Armagnac itself."

"It can be found," Wolfe said. "I've had it."

"You are lucky. I've never so much as tasted it. Would a Loubère be an acceptable substitute?"

"More than acceptable. With a glass of icewater back, if you please?"

The man brought Joshua his drink in a small snifter and set a pitcher of icewater and a glass beside it. Joshua held out a bill. The bar man didn't take it.

"You're new to the Denbeigh," the bartender said. "I'll present a bill when you leave. Also, this early in the afternoon I'll have to get a note that large changed in the lobby."

"This isn't for the drink," Joshua said. "I'd like to repay you for a few moments of your time, Mister Fitzpatrick."

"Ah?" The white-haired man did not take the bill. "You have the advantage on me, sir."

"My name's Taylor. John Taylor. I was told you're considered the . . . mentor, I suppose might be the word, for barmen here on Garrapata."

"A compliment carries its own gold. Your money remains your own, Mister Taylor."

"A Mister Jalon Kakara drinks here when he comes down from Nepenthe."

"Common knowledge," Fitzpatrick said. "He's not a secretive man. Not in that respect, at any rate. That information is hardly worth the sum you're offering."

"I have heard it said that he is, let's say, not the most congenial company when he's displeased."

"He would hardly be the first man of means who might be so described," Fitzpatrick said.

"Let me make a couple of assumptions. Since he drinks when he's traveling, I would assume that he drinks when he is on his home planetoid. Since he is rich, I would assume that he doesn't mix his own drinks."

"Again, your money remains your own."

"I'd like to know whether you, perhaps, know of a fellow barman who might have been employed by him on Nepenthe. I'm sure such a man would have fascinating tales."

"He might," Fitzpatrick agreed. "But those tales might not reflect well on his former employer."

"Particularly," Wolfe said flatly, "if Kakara knocked him on his ass when he fired him, or maybe just screamed and generally treated him like a scut."

"Are you writing a book, Mister Taylor?"

"I could be. But I am not."

"You know," Fitzpatrick said thoughtfully, "if you spoke to such a man, if I knew of such a man, you might end up with very damaging information. Someone who didn't wish Mister Kakara well, someone who himself might have felt his wrath as an innocent, might relish such an event coming to pass."

"I'd say so."

Fitzpatrick picked up a pen and notepad from under the bar, wrote swiftly, tore the piece of paper off, and handed it to Wolfe. "Here's an address where you'll find someone who'll be helpful. Give him this note. He'll tell you whatever you might be interested in."

His hand picked up the bill, caressed it.

"Yes," Fitzpatrick said gently. "Mister Kakara being a bit taken aback is something to relish, indeed. Your drink, by the way, Mister Taylor, is on the house."

*

"So Jerry sent you along, eh?" The man yawned once again, then got up from the rumpled sheets that turned the narrow couch into a bed. "I need some coffee if we're going to talk about a turd like Kakara. C'mon in the kitchenette."

Wolfe followed the man through a doorway. There was just room for the two of them. The man filled a small coffeemaker and touched its START stud. Water hissed, and the tiny pot filled with brown liquid.

A starship lifted from the nearby field, and the tiny apartment's walls shuddered slightly. The man turned his head.

"Two weeks, and I'll be off on one of those," he said. "The hell with the Federation. Things're bound to be better out in the Outlaw Worlds. Can't get worse, anyway."

There was a bottle on the sideboard. The man lifted, shook it. "Hell. Isn't even enough for an eye-opener."

"Here. Try some of mine, Mister Hollister." Joshua took a hammered-silver flask from an inside pocket and passed it to the man.

"That's civilized," Hollister said. He found a cup, hesitated, then rinsed it out at the sink, knocking over a couple of the unwashed dishes when he did. "Now, if there's another cup around . . ."

"Just some water," Wolfe said. "It's a little late for coffee for me."

"All right." Hollister cleaned a glass that had A MEMORY OF SHELDON SPRINGS etched into it and gave it to Joshua. He unscrewed the cap of the flask, sniffed, looked surprised. "Lordamercy," he said. "It's almost a shame to pour this on top of the crap I've been drinking lately."

He looked swiftly at Joshua, as if afraid Wolfe was going to agree with him, then poured until his cup was about half full. He added coffee to the mixture, gave the flask back to Wolfe.

Joshua poured two fingers into the glass, then added water from the tap.

They went back into the main room. Hollister pushed the sheets off the end of the couch, sat, and indicated a chair. Wolfe sat, putting his glass carefully on a rickety table.

"I owe Jerry large," Hollister said. "And maybe I'd like to come back this way again if things don't work out, out there, so I'll give you whatever you want as a favor. What do you need?"

"Nobody's asking for a free ride," Joshua said. He took out a bill, folded it in half, and set it on the table.

"For that," Hollister said, "you can brainscan me about Kakara and damn near anything else. What do you need?"

"You were on Nepenthe?"

"There, and two or three times he told me to go with him on that tub of his, the *Laurel*. Mister, I hope you're planning to do some serious damage to Kakara. I'd call him a prick, but that's the best part of a man, and he doesn't qualify in my eyes. The only person he treats worse'n the help is that poor goddamned wife of his.

"What're you going to do to him?"

Wolfe shook his head. "I'm just interested in hearing some stories. No more, no less."

Hollister looked disappointed; he drank about half of what was in the cup.

"The first thing I'd like to know is how you got the job," Wolfe said.

"First question you ought to ask," Hollister said, "is *why* I got so friggin' dumb as to want it in the first place. But I'll start where you told me."

* * *

"All right," the woman snapped. "You. Taylor. Get in here."

Joshua obediently stood, moved out of the row he sat in, past the knees of the other waiting men and women, and followed the woman into her office.

She slammed the door hard.

"What in the hell makes you think a good man like Mister Jalon Kakara would ever be interested in hiring you?"

"Perhaps," Joshua said calmly, "because I'm one of the best bartenders in the Federation."

"You say that. But I looked at your fiche. God's blazes, you've got a better record as a vagrant than a barman. Looks like you've worked on a dozen worlds or more. Haven't you ever heard of job stability? That's what employers really want."

"I haven't found any problem getting work," Wolfe

said, his tone still unruffled. "Perhaps my trade has different standards than what you're accustomed to."

"Like hell," the woman said. "I've been running an employment agency for twenty years, so don't tell me what I'm accustomed to and what I'm not. Taylor, I wouldn't even bother calling Mister Kakara's personnel director about someone like you. Pity's sakes, I'm surprised I'm not thinking about calling Customs and asking why the hell you were allowed on Garrapata, anyway."

"I'm sorry to have taken your time," Joshua said, and stood.

His hand was on the sensor when the woman spoke again. "Mister Taylor, would you wait for a moment?"

Wolfe turned around. The woman's entire manner had changed.

"Would you please accept my apology for my atrocious behavior?"

Wolfe put surprise on his face. "Of course."

"Would you sit down, please, sir? And could I get you something to drink?"

"No. No, thank you." Wolfe returned to his chair. "But could I ask what's going on? This entire interview has been *very* irregular."

"You certainly may. And I'd appreciate it if what I say not go out of here. When you came in, saying you understood my agency hires experienced service personnel, and that you further understood Jalon Kakara was one of my clients, and you were interested in entering his employ, I, quite frankly, wanted to just ignore you.

"But Mister Kakara pays me well. And often," the woman added, a note of bitterness in her voice, "as he damned well should, considering the number of people he goes through.

"The reason I behaved like an utter bitch, Mister Taylor, is that Kakara is one of the most unpleasant beings I've ever had the misfortune to have as a client. I like to form a long-term relationship with my employees, since as you well know there aren't very many good ones in the service sector. Least of all"—and she tapped Wolfe's carefully forged resume—"ones with your credentials and capabilities, which, of course, I'm actually most impressed by.

"So I determined to test you, to see if I thought you might be able to survive working for him. If you'd shouted back at me, or told me you thought I was an evil-behaved slut, I would have apologized, explained, and then found you another place to work where you'd be far happier. But you appear to have the skin of a rhinoceros and the patience of a saint.

"Now do you understand why I acted as I did?"

"I do. You needn't apologize any further. I've already been told Mister Kakara can be difficult."

"Not can be. *Is.* Almost all the time. Do you still wish to work for him?"

"I do."

"Could I be nosy, and wonder why?"

"Perhaps because of the challenge," Wolfe said.

"I've heard," the woman said, carefully looking away from Joshua, "that Kakara doesn't much care about what someone did before he arrives on Nepenthe. He feels he's his own law and can handle anything that happens on his world. He doesn't need to pay much attention to anyone else's laws . . . or to their outlaws."

"Is that right?" Wolfe's voice was mildly interested.

The woman stared hard at him, and he returned her gaze, his expression bland, closed.

* CHAPTER FOUR *

Nepenthe had been built during the war, for the war, by its money, and when the war and the money ran out, it'd been abandoned as quickly as the nameless ten-mile-long chunk of igneous rock had swarmed with workers after the first Al'ar raid into the Federation.

It had been moved from its original orbit into a Lagrangian point off Garrapata and its rotation had been stilled. The planetoid was named ODS(M) (S)-386 and was ready to be fanged.

The sunward face of the moonlet was studded with solar energy cells, and the receptors were shielded. On the "outward"-facing surface, where a jutting crag spoiled the illusion of a beef tenderloin abandoned on a grill, the rock had been cut away and a small domed outpost built.

The top of the crag was beveled flat, and the tiny world's single weapon installed there. It was a massive sun gun, hardly the most sophisticated of weapons but effective in defense, and was manned by hastily trained Garrapatian recruits.

Orbital Defense System (Manned) (Solar) Number 386. Other planets in the Federation were given equivalent defense systems, while the Outlaw Worlds, officially called the Frontier Systems, were ignored, left open to not infrequent Al'ar assaults and even conquest.

With peace, no one wanted or needed ODS(M) (S)-386, but it was only abandoned for three years. Jalon Kakara needed a base for his merchant fleet, where the hastily converted transports wouldn't be troubled with registry, safety, or crewing regulations.

The barracks area was extended and became first docks, then shipyards. On the far side of the peak the sun gun had once topped, converters churned the rock into soil, added nutrients, and a park was sculpted. Then the entire planetoid was domed and given an atmosphere.

Where the sun gun had been, Kakara built his great palace. Energy was free, and so antigrav generators held the soaring, sweeping arcs of buildings, terraces, and decks above the ground's defiling touch, curving ramps connecting them, a dream of flight in stone and steel.

On one of those terraces Joshua Wolfe, obsequious in white coat, black trousers, and a disarming smile, polished the last glass until it gleamed, and set it with its brothers on a shelf.

He was on a verandah that opened on a swimming pool artfully made of rock so it looked like a sinuous forest pond. To his right was the lushness of Kakara's park, to the left the black-and-gray industrial boil of Nepenthe's heart.

Above and behind him, accessible by a seemingly unguarded ramp, were the multilevel rooms that made up Jalon Kakara and his wife's private apartments.

He had been on Nepenthe for almost a month and had yet to meet his master.

"Hey, friend. How's about some service?" The voice was, at the same time, tough and tentative.

The man it belonged to was medium size, overweight, and wore a lounging suit that had been custom-made for a bigger man, then hastily retailored.

"Good morning, Mister Oriz."

The man eyed him with the cold look of a toad considering a fly's vitamin content. "You know me, eh?"

"Yes, sir. The agency was kind enough to provide a description of all members of Mister Kakara's immediate staff."

"First mistake, Taylor. You *are* Taylor, right? I ain't staff. I'm Mister Kakara's friend. That's all." The cold eyes waited to be believed, looked away when they were satisfied, then returned to check.

Wolfe had been warned about Jack Oriz. Friend he might have been, as much as Kakara recognized the term. He also provided security for the magnate and, like many hangers-on, had a fine-honed sense of paranoia. One of the maids had said Oriz's first name had been different, but he'd changed it to wear Kakara's monogrammed hand-me-downs.

"My apologies, sir."

"Too early to drink?"

"The sun's up, sir. And I'm on duty. What can I bring you?"

"You know how to do a Frost Giant?"

"Yes, sir."

Wolfe took five bottles from a freeze cabinet, poured measured amounts into a double-walled glass, then unlocked another cabinet. He pulled on insulated gloves, took out a flask, opened it, and with tongs dropped a purple-streaked, hissing bit of nastiness into the mixture. What appeared to be flame shot up, then swirling mists rose around it.

He set it in front of Oriz with a flourish.

"Not bad," the man said without the slightest note of approval. "Mix yourself whatever you're having." It wasn't a suggestion.

Wolfe refilled his coffee mug.

"Don't drink on the job, eh?"

"I don't drink at all, sir."

"Another one of the reformed ones."

"No, sir. Never started."

"Then how'd you end up doing what you're doing?" Oriz asked.

"My mother owned five bars, so I grew up in the business."

"What happened?"

"The war."

Oriz grunted, lost interest. "What do you think of working here?"

"So far, it's a good job, sir. I'm looking forward to meeting Mister Kakara."

"Yeah, well, our business took a little longer than we thought. Jalon'll throw himself a welcome-home party tonight. You'll meet him then. It'll probably get wild."

Wolfe shrugged. "It's his world, and I'm drawing his silver. Why not?"

"Maybe you haven't seen real wild. You ever heard the joke about Jalon, the two whores, and the Chitet?"

He told it. The story was improbable, obscene, and made Kakara out as a sex-happy fool. Wolfe had heard it three times before on other worlds, each time with a different rich man as the center. The first version had involved the Earth-King Henry VIII and a pope.

When Oriz had finished, he laughed loudly, his eyes never leaving Joshua's face. Wolfe permitted himself a polite chuckle.

Oriz finished the last of his drink, stood.

"Another, sir?"

"More than one of those every couple hours and the party'll have to start without me. Besides, I got work to do." He turned and waddled away. He veered slightly to the side once, almost slipping into the pool, corrected his course, and vanished down one of the ramps.

Wolfe looked thoughtfully after him, then knelt and began checking the underside of the bar's shelves. He found what he was looking for under the bottom one. It was a gray-green ovoid, a phrase-activated surveillance bug.

"Very cute," he said below a whisper. "Say the secret word or retell Oriz's little story, and win a thumping.

"I *am* looking forward to meeting you, Mister Kakara."

*

It was late.

The series of rooms set aside for the party were packed. Joshua wondered where all the people had come from. Not even a yacht as big as the *Laurel* could have held them all. He'd seen a few of them in Kakara's absence, wandering around the sprawling mansion, planets without a system.

Now the sun had returned, and the magnate's well-paid friends swirled about him. The music that boomed around Wolfe as he made his way through the crowd, balancing a tray of champagne flutes, came from a quartet on a platform halfway up one wall. It was supposed to be Indian skitch, he guessed, its edges rounded by the distance from New Calcutta, the mediocrity of the musicians, and the tastes of the audience. Joshua thought wryly that the two or three dozen people present who might've been young enough to like the real stuff were more likely to bat their eyes and prefer the tastes—in everything—of their older and richer "friends."

He moved around a woman who was leaning against a replica of Michelangelo's *Victory* and staring contemptuously at a man sprawled on the floor at her feet. Someone had scrawled KAKARA RULES on the conqueror's knee.

Two women in old-fashioned tuxedoes were dancing skillfully with each other.

An old man sat backward in a Chippendale chair, maneuvering a model of a *de Ruyter*–class monitor around as if he were ten years old.

A man Wolfe noted for his classically handsome features was holding an intense conversation with the dancer in a Degás painting Joshua was fairly sure was real.

A troupe of ignored acrobats arced back and forth near the ceiling like playful swallows.

Joshua heard Kakara's voice before he saw him. It was loud, commanding, its edges blurred a little by alcohol.

"Damned straight she packed it in on you," he said. "You took her away from Potrero, di'n't you? Woman that's got her eye on the main chance, hell, she'll walk from you the minute she sees better. You were just the thing of the moment, just like Dardick or whatever his name is'll be the next on the list when she starts lookin' again.

"No wonder your da asked me to put you right. You

got some kind of idea people do things for good reasons rather than because they just want to or because they've got any choice in the matter."

Kakara wore black dress trousers with a black silk stripe up the side and a collarless silk shirt that had the Kakara house emblem, the jagged red lightning streak, in place of a neckcloth, no jacket. He was berating a slender man about half his age, who wore more conventional formal dress.

Standing around Kakara, nodding at appropriate intervals, were five other men and Oriz.

To one side was the small woman with dark hair whose picture Joshua had seen in Cormac's office. Her eyes were a little glazed, and she held a glass without appearing to notice it was empty.

Wolfe lowered the tray and stood unobtrusively to the side while Kakara continued:

"I'm sorry. But if you run across someone who's important to you—like Rita is to me—you make sure they don't get an opportunity to go in harm's way. It's the best for all concerned."

He turned to the dark-haired woman and waited. After an interval, she nodded. He turned back, seemingly satisfied.

"Boy, you should count this a good lesson. Let's face it, that woman wasn't anything special. So she was pretty, so she did whatever she did to you in bed that set your little wick wiggling.

"You're rich, boy. You're going to learn there's a million more where she came from. Thing that's important, like I said, is to keep it from happening again. Not just with women, but with everybody.

"You find somebody you need—I mean, really need—you fasten 'em to you with whatever it takes. Money. Position. Power. Whatever. You make double-dogged sure they can't get a better deal elsewhere.

"Or, and this can be the most important thing, don't let 'em think they can do better. Make 'em afraid to start looking. Keep them tied to you, as long as you need them. That's the way to keep people loyal. And I'm pretty damned good at it."

He spun suddenly and looked at Wolfe. "Aren't I?"

"I assume so, sir," Joshua said quietly.

"Assume? Don't you *know*?"

"I haven't been in your employ long enough to form an opinion. Sir."

Kakara snorted. "Opinions are like assholes. Everybody has one, and it's for sale. Right?"

Joshua kept the smile in place, said nothing.

"You're just like the others," Kakara said. He reached out, took a flute from Wolfe's tray, drained it. He was about to turn, stopped, frowned, and his eyes held Joshua's.

They flickered away, and he shook his head, as if he'd just had a glass of icewater tossed in his face.

"No," he said in a low voice. "No, you're not."

Joshua put a quizzical look on his face, nodded, and slipped off.

*

The dark-haired woman leaned back against the ten-foot-high chunk of driftwood that had been stained, lacquered, and declared art. She was looking out and down at the flaring lights along a shipway as construction robots crawled and welded. She didn't appear to be seeing them.

Joshua moved up beside her. Now his tray held an assortment of small liqueur glasses.

"Would you care for a drink, Captain Sidamo?"

The woman started, looked at him. Her face hardened. "My name is Mrs. Kakara," she said. "Are you making some sort of joke?"

"No, ma'am."

"Are you one of Oriz's amateur spies? Or is my husband playing games again?"

"The bridge of the *PC-1186*," Wolfe said. "Cormac said you would remember that. You won't remember me, but I remember you. You were his logistics officer and I was one of his . . . clients every now and then. I don't think we ever were introduced."

Once more Rita Kakara showed surprise. She looked about hastily. "Careful. There are bugs everywhere."

"Not here."

"How do you know?"

"There was one behind that chunk of wood. I deactivated it an hour ago." Wolfe didn't wait for a response. "Now. Reach out, take one of the glasses. Taste it. You hate it. Give it back to me, and I am going to suggest another one, pointing at each."

The woman hesitated, then obeyed.

"You're genuine," she murmured. "Did Cormac tell you what happened that afternoon on the patrol craft?"

"No. I didn't figure it was any of my business."

"He always was a gentleman." A smile touched her lips, and she was suddenly as young as Wolfe remembered her. "Can you get me out?"

"I'm going to try."

"When? How?"

"I don't know yet," Wolfe said. "But keep your track shoes handy . . . and this liqueur, Mrs. Kakara, is Deneb Reducto. It's brandy that's had most of the water taken out and replaced with an herbal compound."

Oriz was at his elbow. "Jalon sent me over," he said to Rita. "He said to remind you it'll be a long day tomorrow."

Rita moved her face into the semblance of a smile. "How thoughtful of Jalon," she said. "I certainly wouldn't want a hangover. Thank you, Jack.

"I don't believe I'll try any of your wares, sir. That first taste should have warned me."

Wolfe offered the tray to Oriz, who eyed him, then shook his head.

Wolfe bowed and moved toward a group of three men.

*

Joshua slid the rack of glasses into the washer, closed the door and touched the sensor. Steam boiled out, and he began loading another rack.

"Leave that," a voice ordered. "I need a drink."

It was Jalon Kakara, appearing no drunker, no soberer than he had before.

"Yes, sir. What may I get you?"

There was a pale light from outside as the planetoid's program suggested dawn was close.

"In the back cabinet, there's a bottle. No label. I'll take about four fingers of it."

Wolfe found a dark-brown bottle, poured a clear, colorless fluid, and passed it across. The big man warmed the glass in the palms of his hands, then sniffed deeply.

"Might I inquire as to what that is, sir?"

"On the world I come from, the government sets high duty on any alcohol. So we build our own. I keep some on hand."

"Is it good?"

"Hell no! It's swill. I keep it around to remind me of . . . of certain things."

Kakara drank, set the glass down with a clatter. "So you don't think everyone's got a price, as does everything they believe, eh?"

"I didn't say that. Since I'm on your payroll I'd sound like several species of a fool if I did," Wolfe replied.

"But you don't think that what people believe is on the block?"

"Sometimes," Wolfe answered. "Sometimes not. Sometimes it doesn't cost anything, either. People have a pretty good way of convincing themselves what they ought to believe at any given time without much encouragement."

"Shit! Philosophy."

Wolfe shook his head. "Not at all, sir. Just talking about what I've seen."

"The philosopher barman," Kakara said. A corner of his mouth twisted.

He drained the glass, got up. "Maybe I better keep you close. Find out more about what you think. That'd give you a chance to see whether I'm good at writing the music and then making anyone around me dance to it—and like it."

"As you wish, sir."

Kakara looked appraisingly at Wolfe, then slid off the bar stool and walked away.

Wolfe watched until he'd left the big room, then went back to stacking glasses in the wash rack.

His expression was thoughtful.

*

Joshua lay on a knoll in the center of the planetoid's park, on a towel. There were sandals, a pullover, knee-shorts beside him, and he had another towel over his hips. His eyes were closed.

He was not asleep. He floated out, away, toward the invisible roof of the planetoid, where the artificial sun and clouds floated.

His fingers were splayed, thumb and forefinger touching, resting gently on his stomach.

I float . . . I see . . . the void around me . . . all elements are one . . . I feel the world about me . . . I reach, do not reach, for a way, for a place, where I may call, where the woman and I may flee from . . . the void . . . the emptiness . . . I bring nothing . . . I take nothing . . .

He *felt* someone's eyes on him, sat up slowly, yawning.

Rita Kakara left the path below the knoll and walked toward him. She wore a yellow sundress and was barefoot. Her feet made small springy indentations in the thick turf.

"Good afternoon, Mister 'Taylor.' " The quotes she put around Wolfe's name were barely noticeable.

"Mrs. Kakara."

"I suppose you've heard already."

"No, ma'am. I've heard nothing. I haven't checked in today. I'm on the late shift."

"Not anymore you're not. My husband's changed your assignment."

"Oh?"

"He wants you to take charge of the bar on the *Laurel*. The bar and the commissary. Your contract will be adjusted accordingly."

Wolfe rubbed his chin, thinking. "Thank you," he said. "I gather it's a promotion."

"It is. Even if it'll put you a bit closer to the fire."

"I don't understand."

"My husband doesn't handle travel well. Sometimes he becomes . . . upset easily. Too easily." Rita looked about. "Is it all right to talk?"

Wolfe was about to say yes, but the Lumina concealed in its pouch in his crotch warmed. He shook his head, slightly. The dark-haired woman didn't catch the gesture, started to say more. Wolfe held out a hand, low, palm flat.

"Sorry," she said. "What I meant to say was that Jalon is a little sensitive about this. Some people might find it amusing that a man who made his riches as he did would have problems in space, and think he's afraid.

"That's not it at all." Rita was talking a little too fast, Wolfe thought. But she wasn't doing a bad job of recovery.

"I think it's just that he likes his comforts, his own place, and sometimes isn't aware of it. The reason I wanted to mention it to you is to ask that you not judge him harshly if he snaps at you.

"Please don't take it personally."

"Mrs. Kakara, I do appreciate your taking the time, and I'll certainly do my best. I must say that so far the job has been such a pleasure that something as minor as that won't give me a problem at all."

"I thought you'd understand." She smiled and went back down the path.

Wolfe lay back down, then, after a moment, rolled onto his stomach. He remained motionless, and, after a space, his back moved slowly, regularly.

I look . . . my eyes are many . . . I see . . . I feel . . .

He *felt* a direction but made no move.

A few minutes later, he opened his eyes a slit.

To his right, on a hilltop nearer the mansion that overlooked the knoll, he saw a heavyset, medium-size man who moved like Jack Oriz walk away. Over his shoulder he carried a tripod, with what might have been a spyeye or directional mike mounted on it.

"Grayle, Grayle, *are you listening?*"

The response came through his bones, from the transponder against his breastbone:

"I am."

"Instructions. I shall be leaving this burrow aboard a ship. Follow. Do not allow yourself to be perceived. Stand by for immediate closure and boarding. Give this information to Taen. Clear."

"Understood."

Joshua took off the transponder and replaced it in the cutout copy of *The Barman's Guide to Fine Spirits.*

*

Joshua made a last check on the storage room, closed the door, and went to an intercom. "Commissary to bridge. All items safely stowed."

There was a double-click of acknowledgment.

Joshua went to one of the couches in the barroom, sat down, and leaned back.

Fifteen minutes later, a loudspeaker came on:

"All stations, all stations. Stand by for lift . . . five, four, three, two . . . we're gone."

He *felt* beyond, outside, and *watched* as the *Laurel* came clear of the dock and moved toward the sky, and the illusion of a world vanished.

A great port opened, and the ship went out into blackness, then through the second lock, and was in the utter night/day of space.

Again the loudspeaker spoke:

"Time to jump, four seconds . . . three . . . two . . . one . . . now!"

The *Laurel* was somewhere else.

*

Wolfe heard an argument, then a blow. He looked up from the lemon he was peeling into a long curlicue and saw Rita Kakara stumble into the room, then down the corridor that led to the owner's suite. After a moment, Kakara followed, pausing only to glower at the two men at the bar.

"You didn't see anything," Oriz advised.

"Of course not," Wolfe agreed.

*

"Mister Trang, what's our destination?" Wolfe said.

"Offaly 18," the ship's officer said. "Not that it should matter to you. There'll be no leave granted, which is Mister Kakara's general policy, even his wife.

"Sorry, buster. You don't get the Grand Tour on his credits."

*

"Since you like white wine, Mrs. Kakara, here's something you might not be aware of."

"Oh?" Rita pretended interest.

"It's a Château Felipe, from Rice XIX. Not that dry, very fruity, a bit of—"

The man beside her grabbed a handful of mixed nuts from the bowl on the bar, picked up his drink, and left.

"We're playing it by ear," Wolfe said. "I'm going to try to take you off as soon as we land. Do what I tell you, when I tell it to you. Wear shoes you can run in, clothes that won't stand out. *Don't* bring any baggage or a big handbag. No more jewelry than you usually wear."

"The only thing I want out of this nightmare is me," Rita said. "And you don't have to worry that I'm going to behave like some flip-headed porcelain doll. I'll carry my own weight."

Wolfe nodded once. "Sorry. I *was* selling you . . . and Cormac . . . short."

*

"Open the mike to Taen." Wolfe spoke in Al'ar.

"I am listening," the Al'ar said.

"Here is what passes for a plan. It does not appear we shall be able to get the person we want away from the ship. Nor will I be permitted to leave. The best idea my brain provides is that we bring the Grayle in directly behind the Laurel as it's on final approach. Find out what dock it's going to be landed at, then put some covering fire down, while the woman and I—"

"Don't even breathe heavy," a voice behind him said.

Wolfe spun.

The door to his compartment was open. Standing in it were Oriz and two other men. Oriz held a blaster leveled on Joshua's chest.

Oriz stepped forward, ripped the bonemike off Wolfe's chest, and smashed it with a bootheel.

"It appears you aren't nearly as cute as you think you are, hey?"

*

Kakara hit Wolfe in the side of the head with the flat of a blaster, considered a moment, then hit him again.

Joshua's knees buckled, and he sagged back against the bulkhead. The right side of his face was a mask of blood.

He forced himself erect.

There were five others in the lavish suite: Kakara, Oriz, two bodyguards, and the ship's first officer, Trang.

"You aren't the first who's tried to pull something," Kakara said. "And I'm real sure you aren't going to be the last.

"What was the scheme? Who were you talking to?"

Wolfe didn't answer. Kakara started to hit him again, then turned to the officer.

"Trang, are you *sure* there's no other ships within range?"

"Yessir. We checked all frequencies, all wavelengths. Nothing."

"Then who the hell was he talking to? Somebody on the ship?"

"Unlikely," the sailor answered. "That's a long-range transmitter he was using. Maybe, if it hadn't gotten smashed, I could've figured out something from whatever frequency it was set on. But . . ." He didn't finish.

The door slid open and Rita Kakara entered. She saw Wolfe's swollen face, masked her reaction.

"Rita, get out of here," Kakara said. "This isn't for you."

"Why not? Whatever this man wanted to do . . . wouldn't it have involved me? I want to watch whatever happens to him."

"You think you do now," Oriz said. "But you won't in a little bit."

"Shut up, Jack. Rita can stay if she wants," Kakara said. "But I don't want to hear you sniveling to show him any mercy. The son of a bitch—and his friends—wouldn't have shown us any."

He hefted the gun and stepped toward Wolfe, then stopped. "Jack. Let me borrow your penknife."

Oriz took a small, ivory-bolstered knife from his pocket, opened it, and handed it to Kakara.

The shipline owner grinned, showing all his teeth. It wasn't a nice smile. "Taylor, you ever see what a knife— a little bitty knife like this one—can do?

"I grew up hard, in the yards. The macs liked blades. Kept their women in hand. I saw what can be done . . . when you work slowly enough. Anyone'll tell . . . or do . . . anything."

He licked his lips, set the pistol down on a table, and walked toward Joshua.

The Lumina warmed against Joshua's skin.

Wolfe's form wavered, vanished.

Trang shouted surprise.

The air blurred, and Wolfe was there, heel hand striking Kakara on the forehead. He stumbled back against the table, sending the pistol spinning to the deck.

Trang took three fast steps to the door; he was reaching for its control, when Wolfe knocked him down with a spin-kick and moved on, without finishing him.

A gun went off, and part of a bulkhead sizzled, charred.

Oriz had a hand inside his jacket, reaching for his gun.

Joshua slammed into him, and he crashed into his two henchmen.

Joshua was turning, inside their guard. A backhand rapped one of the men between the eyes; the man squealed and fell, both hands trying to put his face back together, gun dropping, forgotten.

The second man jumped back, let Oriz go down, and was in a fighting stance. Joshua snap-kicked, took him in the elbow. The man yelped, grabbed himself, took a knuckle-strike to the temple, and fell.

Oriz was scrabbling for his gun when Rita kicked him in the side. He grunted, rolled away.

Rita had his gun in both hands.

Kakara had come back to his feet. Rita was between Wolfe and her husband. Oriz pulled himself up.

"Rita! Give me the gun," Kakara snapped.

"I'll get it. She won't shoot," Oriz said

The heavyset man had taken two steps when Rita shot him in the throat, blowing most of his spine into white fragments against the bulkhead. His head flopped once, and he fell forward.

The gun turned, and its bell-mouth held steady on Jalon Kakara.

He lifted two hands, trying to push death away.

"No."

Wolfe's voice was soft.

Rita didn't move. She looked at Joshua, then back at Kakara. Her finger was firm on the firing stud.

Kakara made an unpleasant sound in his throat.

The dark-haired woman turned, tossed the weapon to Wolfe.

He caught it in midair. "Now, let's go have a talk with the bridge about meeting some friends."

*

Wolfe knelt in the open lock, holding the blast rifle that had been waiting in the *Grayle*'s lock on Kakara, the *Laurel*'s captain, and another officer. The side of his face was swollen, the blood only half dried.

"All right, Rita," he said, his voice a little mushy. "I have them. Go on into the ship."

The woman put the safety on her blaster, started to obey, then walked over to Kakara.

The two stared at each other for a very long time.

Kakara was the first to look away.

Rita nodded, as if something had been settled between them, and went quickly into the *Grayle*.

"My ship's armed," Wolfe said. "Cut your losses, Kakara. Don't try to be cute."

The big man stared at him.

"Whoever you are," he said hoarsely. "You better learn to sleep with one eye open. And don't make any long-range investments."

"I never do," Wolfe said. "And I sleep with both eyes open. Always." He slid one hand free, touched the lock sensor, and the door closed.

A clang came as the *Grayle* disconnected from the *Laurel*.

"Sir, shall we track them?"

Jalon Kakara didn't answer. His eyes were still fixed on the blank alloy portal of the airlock.

* CHAPTER FIVE *

"You have no crew?" Rita said.

"Don't much need one. The ship's automated."

"So where was it hiding?"

"Dead astern of the *Laurel*. She doesn't have much of a silhouette anyway, and nobody ever looks over his shoulder. Except in the romances to make sure the wolves are still there."

Rita tried a smile, which graduated to a successful grin. Wolfe poured her another cup of coffee.

"Should I have shot him?" she asked.

"No."

"Why not? The bastard gave me more than my share of bruises. Broken bones, twice. And if you were one of Cormac's people, you surely aren't a pacifist."

"No," Wolfe said, taking his cup to the washer. "I'm hardly that. But death's a little final, sometimes."

*

The planetoid of Malabar, and its attendant junkyard, was "below" them.

The woman eyed the screen.

"Eleven . . . almost twelve years," she mused. "I hope

I haven't built up something to be more than what it was."

"Not from Cormac's lights. And if it is . . . you can always leave."

"No," Rita said flatly. "Maybe I don't know what I should be wanting. I certainly didn't when I went for Jalon.

"I'll stay the course, if he'll have me. Because I know nobody ever, not *ever*, gets a third chance."

*

"I . . . we owe you big," Cormac said.

"You surely do."

"Is there anything you need?"

Wolfe thought, smiled quietly. "A time machine, maybe."

Cormac looked at him. "How far back would you go and change things?"

Wolfe started to answer, stopped. "Maybe . . . all the way back to—" He broke off and said no more.

*

The port slid closed, and Wolfe went up the circular staircase to the control room. **"You may emerge from your burrow."**

A panel slid open, and Taen came out.

"My apologies," Wolfe said in Terran, then switched to Al'ar. **"I have no pride in having to hide you like this."**

"It matters not," the Al'ar said. "I am relieved, in fact, because I do not have to injure my sensors with the sight of more humans. Now, have we adequately fulfilled the role of Noble Savior?"

"For the moment," Wolfe said. "And thanks for your appreciation for humanity."

"This was received," Taen said, pointing to a screen. "I do not know how to decode it, but I suspect it is the response from the Federation Intelligence man."

Wolfe went to the screen and studied the message for awhile.

"Cisco is depending one hell of a lot on my memory," he muttered. "It's an old hasty code we used during the war. I think. Let's see . . . OX4YM, RYED3 . . . I can't do it in my head anymore."

He opened a drawer, took out a pad and pencil, began scrawling. Twice he got up to consult star charts on a screen.

"All right," he said after some time. "I think I have it. Most of it, anyway, and I can guess the rest. It *was* from Cisco, and it was setting up a meeting. We've got about two E-weeks to make it, with five days slop on either side.

"I think it's pretty safe. Cisco's going to set his ship down on an armpit called Yerkey's Planet. It's a single-planet system, with not much of anywhere to hide. If we can make a slow approach, ready to streak like a scalded cat if anything flickers . . . maybe. Just maybe.

"Ship. Take us out of this junkyard. Make two blind jumps when we have room, and put us somewhere in empty space, and I'll give you the ana/kata numbers at that time."

"Understood."

The *Grayle* lifted away from Malabar under medium drive.

Two minutes off, the emergency com frequency

blared. "Unknown ship, unknown ship. Cut drive, stand by to be inspected."

"Ship! All weapons systems on standby."

"Understood."

Wolfe swung down a mike. "This is the yacht *Otranto*, broadcasting on standard emergency frequency. Identify yourself, and give authority for your request."

"Otranto, this is the *Ramee*. We made no request but demand you stand by for inspection. We are in pursuit of a dangerous Federation criminal."

"Ship," Wolfe said, "give me any specs on the *Ramee*."

"No ship of that name found."

"Do you have any entry, anywhere, on the name *Ramee*?"

"Otranto, Otranto, this is the *Ramee*. Be advised we are armed, and will launch to disable unless you communicate instantly and cut your drive. Do not attempt to enter N-space. We will match orbit."

"Ramee," the ship said calmly. *"More commonly known as Petrus Ramus. An eminent logician. A native of ancient Earth, of the country then known as France. Most noted—"*

"Stop," Wolfe said. "With a name like that, a Chitet?"

Taen moved his grasping organs. "From what you have told me, it would make sense that they would name their spacecraft after thinkers," Taen said. "Hardly a subtle maneuver, however."

"Doubt if they care, this far from anything." Wolfe keyed the mike. "*Ramee*, this is the *Otranto*. I must protest this piracy in the strongest terms. There is no one on board this craft but the captain and four crew members. We are delivering this craft to its new owners on Rialto."

"This inspection will take only a few moments. Stand by. We will be sending a team across as soon as we are in conjunction with you."

"So much for an honest face," Wolfe said. "Ship, do you have any ID on the *Ramee* from its dimensions?"

"The ship resembles three classes of vessels. However, two of them are rare prototypes, so it is most likely the ship is a somewhat modified Requesans-*class destroyer built by the Federation. I display its possible weaponry, performance."*

Wolfe scanned the screen. "Fast little bastard. Fine. Ship, give me a screen with the *Ramee* on it and its probable orbit in relation to us."

Another screen lit. The Chitet craft, four times the size of the *Grayle*, was closing on the *Grayle* from directly "ahead."

"Cautious, ain't they? Ship, dump one missile out of the tubes. Do not activate drive, do not activate homing system, maintain on standby."

"Understood."

"At my command, you will go to full secondary drive. Put us as close to the *Ramee* as you can. As soon as you clear the other ship, activate the missile behind us and home it on the *Ramee*. Then take us back toward Malabar. I want an orbit that closely intersects the abandoned ships, emerges on the far side of the planet."

"Understood."

Breathe . . . breathe . . . reach . . .

Wolfe felt the Al'ar beside him stir.

Fire, burn . . .

"Ship, go!"

Drive-hum built around him. Wolfe had an instant to see the *Ramee* blur up onscreen, *felt* it pass, then, in a rear screen, saw the computer-created flare that represented his missile as its drive cut in and it shot toward the Chitet starship.

Ahead, the clutter of Malabar loomed.

"The Ramee *has launched three countermissiles. One miss . . . one bypass . . . third missile impacted. Our missile destroyed."*

"I guess we couldn't hope to surprise them like we did the *Ashida*," Wolfe complained. "Ship, how long on the far side of Malabar will we be able to jump?"

"At full secondary power, seventy-three minutes."

"What's the status on the *Ramee*?"

"It has recovered and has set an intersecting orbit. My systems indicate it is preparing to launch an attack."

"I thought they wanted us alive."

"If these Chitet are not experienced soldiers," Taen said, "perhaps they have great faith their weapons will do exactly as they wish and only cripple this ship and leave us to be captured."

Wolfe managed a grin. "Yeah. I believed that, too, once. But I'd just as soon not help them learn a missile's about as selective as a hand grenade in a nursery most times. Not when I'm about to be the dissatisfied consumer."

*"Ramee *has launched. Three missiles. Probability of impact . . . fifty-three percent, plus or minus five percent."*

"I guess we made them lose their temper. Pisspoor for folks who like to think they're cool, calm, and collected. Put us on an intersection orbit with the boneyard . . . correction, those abandoned ships."

"Understood."

"Give me a close-up screen."

The ship obeyed. Wolfe looked at the blips.

"Ship, set a direct collision course for the biggest of the ships."

"Understood."

Once more the drive hummed.

"On command, I want you to change orbit radically, any direction, hold new course for three seconds, then return to previous course passing us close to Malabar."

"Understood."

The ships and their parent planetoid were scattered hundreds of miles apart, but on Wolfe's screen, and in his mind, that part of space was as crowded as any ocean harbor.

"Ship, what's the impact time on those missiles?"

"Twenty-six seconds."

"When do we collide with the ship you're aiming at?

"Twenty-nine seconds."

"At twenty seconds, obey my orders."

"Understood."

Wolfe's eyes followed the old-fashioned sweep pointer on the control panel. He could *feel* death close on him, black wolves with muscles of hydrogen ions.

Quite suddenly the ship's drive moaned, and the artificial gravity lost its focus. Wolfe felt "down" move around him, swallowed hard, then everything was normal.

"Missiles evaded."

One screen bloomed violet fire, blanked, and a second, shielded one repeated the view.

The forward half of one of Cormac's mothballed

battleships vanished in a radioactive spray as all three
of the Chitets' missiles struck.

"Well, Cormac did ask if I wanted one," Wolfe said to
himself. "Duped their young asses, we did. Ship, will the
Ramee be able to catch us?"

*"Estimate . . . possibly. But not within time frame you
ordered until jump. However, they are maintaining pursuit. Not likely they will close distance as we pass
through remainder of ships and the planetoid. Estimation
of closest time they will be capable of launching attack:
eighty-seven minutes."*

"Well, thank Sheol for small favors."

Wolfe realized he'd been standing, sagged down into
his chair, massaged aching thigh muscles. He wiped a
sleeve across his forehead, pulled it away wet. He turned
to Taen.

"They *really* don't like us."

"That is something I hope your Cisco can clarify."

"He's got more than that to explain," Wolfe said, a bit
grimly.

*

Wolfe accepted the Lumina's flare, wrapped himself
around it, let the flame become him, and reached out, beyond the spaceship's skin.

Void . . . nothing . . . I accept all . . .

He wasn't sure what he was looking for. Perhaps some
sign of the Guardians they sought, perhaps a homing signal to the Great Lumina that might or might not exist.

He felt an attraction, turned in space.

His focus was abruptly broken, shattered, and he was
back in the bare exercise room.

The Lumina was a dull, egg-shaped gray stone beside him.

All his mind could remember was the sudden angry buzzing, as if a boy had kicked over a hive of bees.

On Wolfe's arm were angry red welts, slowly disappearing.

*

The *Grayle* crept toward the dying red star and the bulk that had been named Yerkey's Planet.

Taen scanned the ship's screens. All were either blank or showed normal readings.

"The time allocated is almost over," he said. "Perhaps Cisco has already departed."

"If so, then he'll try to set the meet up again," Wolfe said. "A good way to keep from springing a trap is to be very early or very late.

"Ship, how close are we to the planet?"

"Three AUs, approximately. Do you wish ETA?"

"Negative. I want a full orbit of the planet before we consider landing. Report any broadcasts on any frequency, any man-made objects observed."

"Understood."

The *Grayle* slid on, all unnecessary systems shut down, its sensors fingering emptiness.

*

"I have one not-natural object located," the ship reported. *"It is a frigate, of the* Jomsviking *class. From its signature we have encountered this ship before."*

"When a man who I called Cisco came aboard about a year ago?"

"Affirmative."

"Can you tell what the frigate's combat status is?"

"Not precisely. No weapons launch points are extruded. Slight discharge from drive tubes detectable, suggesting ship is ready to lift with minimal notice."

"Nothing ventured . . . all right. Take us in on a slow landing orbit. If that ship broadcasts anything, or if you pick up any other sign of artificial presence, drive at full power for space, and enter N-space, blind-jump, as soon as possible."

"Understood."

*

Yellow dust boiled around the *Grayle* as it landed, hung heavily in the thin atmosphere of the low-grav planet.

A man in a suit came out of the Federation frigate's lock, waddled slowly to a point about halfway between the two ships, and waited, listening to the whisper of his suit's air conditioner. After some time, a man in a suit, faceplate darkened, came out of the dust cloud. Wolfe walked to within ten feet of the man, stopped.

"Cisco."

"You have the Al'ar?" the Federation Intelligence executive asked. "Is he on your ship?"

"Seems to me that warrant you put out on me means I'm hardly honor-bound to answer."

"All right," Cisco said. "I did that because I had to. I didn't have any choice."

"People who take up your trade generally use that for an excuse."

"This time it's the truth. The hell with it. I'm assuming you've got the Al'ar and have got some kind of operation going." He held up a gauntleted hand. "Let me come back to that.

"I wanted to tell you you were right. My superiors said those Chitet were renegades. I bought into that. But after what happened at Tworn Station . . . no more."

"Very quick," Wolfe said sarcastically. "What gave you the hint? That there were three of their goddamned ships around? That their president or director or whatever he calls himself—"

"Matteos Athelstan. His title is Master Speaker."

"Right. That he just happened to be at Tworn Station with about a trillion of what a woman called his religious caterpillars when the guns started going off?

"Good, quick analysis, Cisco. No wonder the Federation took six goddamned months to figure out the war had started back then."

"Knock it off, Wolfe. We're all in the dark on this one. You just happened to be the guy on point who set things off."

Wolfe grunted, subsided.

"Fortunately, we were able to cover up what happened down there."

"Why? Why does the Federation give a damn? Why'd you alibi them? Why don't you call up a division or so of the Navy and have them police these clowns up and put thumbscrews on this Athelstan until he sings?"

"Sure," Cisco said. "You've been out here in the Outlaw Worlds too long. The Federation doesn't work like that. Hell, no government does, not and be able to hold together for very long. And sure as hell your average citizen doesn't need to know that one of the most respected groups in civilization, known for quietness, efficiency, honesty, appears to have gone completely amok. We're trying to figure out the whole scope before we take action."

"Meantime, you do nothing."

Cisco made no response.

"All right. Let me take it now. Are you willing to admit there is a conspiracy? That it's a big one?"

Cisco nodded, then realized his motion couldn't be seen through the tiny faceplate and made an agreeing sound.

"You know the Chitet have a man inside Intelligence Directorate?"

"Yes. More than one. I think I can ID two, but there's at least two others," Cisco said. "But it's worse than that. I can't smoke them out because they've got cover farther up."

"Inside the government?"

"Yes."

"High up."

"Yes. And in more than one branch."

Wolfe muttered inaudibly. "What are they after?"

"This is where it gets complicated," Cisco said. "Nobody knows. But I was able to set up a cutout operation and started some archivists digging into what we know about the Chitet, going all the way back."

"Back what, four hundred or so years ago," Wolfe asked, "when they tried their little coup and got their paws slapped?"

He heard a surprised hiss from Cisco's microphone. "There aren't a lot of people who know about that one."

"I read history."

"That's where we started," Cisco went on. "About two hundred years ago, not long after we made first contact with the Al'ar, the Chitet sent out an expedition to make contact with them."

"Why?"

"The few records we've found don't say. And there's not much in the archives—somebody fine-toothed them and got almost everything to the shredder. Almost, but not quite."

"What happened?"

"Something went wrong. They sent seven ships. None of them came back. No known survivors."

"You're saying the Chitet took a hit like that and didn't scream to the government?"

"Exactly," Cisco said. "Obviously they were doing something they didn't want us to learn about. Ever."

"What was their position during the war?" Wolfe asked. "I was out of town and not reading the papers."

"Unsurprisingly, they were fervent backers of the war effort and the government. Ran recruiting drives in their movement, raised money to buy ships, big on the various war bond drives, and so forth. Their then–Master Speaker, not Athelstan, hit the rubber-chicken circuit, always on the same theme: There can be but one imperial race in the galaxy, and it must be Man."

"Well, something changed," Wolfe said. "In case you don't know it, they aren't after your Al'ar to slot him as the last survivor. At Tworn Station they were trying to take him alive."

"That was my estimation," Cisco said. "Otherwise, they would've just dropped one nuke on the lid of that dome and let the ocean in to sort things out."

"Maybe," Wolfe said slowly, "maybe they figure the

Al'ar had something they could use. Something that'd let them pull another coup . . . one that'd succeed this time.

"You know they're buying every old warship they can get their hands on, preferably with the weapons systems intact."

"Shit!" Cisco said. "No. I didn't."

"Now let's get personal. What are you—and FI, at least the part of it that isn't wearing dark suits and thinking logically—doing with me? Using me as your goddamned stalking horse?"

"I considered that," Cisco said. "But they're too close, and there's too many of them. I want to help you in whatever you're trying to do." He gestured at the ship behind him. "You can use me—and the *Styrbjorn*—if you want. But first I wanted to get some of the heat off you.

"I started a disinformation program a couple of months ago. You upped stakes and headed for the other side of the known universe, you've gone to ground inside the Federation, there's stories that your ship blew up, somebody killed you in a gunfight . . . as much as I can plant to confuse the issue."

"Let me tell you something," Wolfe said dryly. "So far your little scheme isn't working. A Chitet ship jumped me when I was offplaneting . . . the last place I was at." He ignored Cisco's start of surprise.

"And you best be careful on your own right," he continued. "Not that I give much of a shit, but if the Chitet inside FI figure out what you're doing, you could end up on the short end of a rope."

"I'm careful," Cisco said. "I'm always careful. I'm using clean cutouts. Like our mutual friend who helped set up the meeting."

"You still haven't answered the question," Wolfe said. "What do you want from me?"

"I want information," Cisco said. His voice rose from his customary monotone. "I'll ask the same questions I did before. What is the Al'ar looking for? Why was he wandering from homeworld to homeworld? Does he know what the Chitet could be after? Come on, Wolfe. I need help."

Wolfe stood motionless for a space, then walked off, toward his ship.

"Wait! Goddammit, Wolfe, this can't be a one-way pipeline!"

Wolfe stopped, didn't turn. "Right now," he said slowly, his voice sounding muffled, "I'll play the hand you dealt. I'll let you know when I need more cards . . . or have something to discard."

He went on, and the form of his suit disappeared into the dust.

Ten minutes later, the ground shook under Cisco's feet. He turned on an outside mike and heard, dimly, the whine of a shipdrive.

The *Grayle* lifted through the dust and soared toward space.

Cisco watched the flare of its drive until it vanished, then walked back to the *Styrbjorn*.

* CHAPTER SIX *

The *Grayle* whispered through the darkness between stars. The only sound, beside the ship hum, was the dry voice of a man dead more than a thousand years:

> *"The trilling wire in the blood*
> *Sings below inveterate scars*
> *And reconciles forgotten wars.*
> *The dance along the artery*
> *The circulation of the lymph*
> *Are figured in the drift of stars . . ."*

Wolfe swung his feet off the bunk, touched the sensor, and the man's dusty voice stopped. He went toward the control room.

*

"I am sorry," the ship said, and Wolfe imagined pique in the synthesized voice, *"but the task you require is beyond my capabilities, even if I were to shut down all non-life-support duties."*

"Disregard. Resume normal functions," Wolfe said. He tapped fingers on the control panel, thinking. "You're sure you haven't got the vaguest idea where these Guardians might be located?"

"As I have said, that was why I was going from home-world to homeworld, seeking clues," Taen said.

Wolfe frowned, then brightened. "What we need is a computer. A *big* goddamned computer."

"There is such a device on Sauros."

"Which you can run?"

"Because I was working directly for the Command On High when I was hunting you, I was given a special, direct access code. I can use that to avoid the computer's safeguards and, from there, should be able to use the device, assuming standard coding, standard controlling," the Al'ar said. "We should have only one problem."

"Yeah. You told me. It'll try to kill us without proper access."

"I do not think the computer itself will attempt our deaths. When our Planners set up these devices, allowing for emergency use, I would assume they thought a user might not have full access information.

"Where the computer will try to kill us is on the way in, I suspect."

"Big difference," Wolfe said. He thought for a space. "Maybe I know a better way. All this one will do is make me feel like a worthless asshole for a week."

*

The bonemike against his chest vibrated.

"No one told this man his brother had been killed by our forces?"

"He was told," Wolfe said shortly. *"He went mad. He retreated into a world where he had not been told."*

"And he is allowed to remain free, to live completely alone? No one in your society has rechanneled his

mind to the truth? Or else, if that is not possible, ended his life as a gift?"

"We aren't as altruistic as the Al'ar," Wolfe said in Terran. *"Now shut the hell up, Taen. Something's wrong."*

The tottering old house was dark, quiet, dead.

Wolfe moved across the street, stopped at the stainless-steel tube that was the mansion's pneumatic delivery system. When he'd last seen it, less than a year earlier, it'd been new. Now its sleekness was marred, gray. Someone had chalked an obscenity on it. Wolfe tried the access door. It had been jammed shut with a stick.

Wolfe went through the sagging gate and up the weed-grown path onto the sagging porch. He touched the com sensor once, then again, waited for almost half an hour.

Breathe . . . the earth reaches up . . . steady, unmoving . . .

He took two small, bent pieces of metal from his belt-pouch, held the knob steady, hissed surprise as the door came open.

A gun came into his hand as he moved to the side and waited. On the other side was nothing but silence. Silence and a familiar, too-sweet stink that rose above the customary smell of decay.

"The man's a rotten housekeeper," he murmured. "But still."

He took a tiny light from his pouch, went quickly through the open door, flattened himself against the wall.

Nothing happened.

He moved his hand down the jam, found raggedness where a jimmy had pried, slid the door almost closed, snapped the light on, swept it around, turned it off.

"Mister Davout," he said loudly. "It's me. Joshua Wolfe."

Silence.

Again, he turned the light on.

The hall was still stacked with years of high-piled coms. Davout had saved everything, from news, to entertainment, to devices in the sure and certain hope that one day his brother would return.

Wolfe moved the beam to illuminate one of the front rooms. Sealed boxes that had held music-fiches had been ripped open and cast aside.

He went down the hall toward the back stairs, keeping close to one wall. He walked in a strange fashion, crouched, centered, each leg sweeping toward the other in an inward arc, foot touching down toe-first, hesitating, then the full weight on the heel and the next leg moving forward.

The kitchen was still stacked with forgotten, unwashed dishes. But no odor came from them. Even the mold that had grown over them like a blanket had withered, died.

Wolfe took a deep breath, held it, then exhaled and started for the stairs.

Davout had cleverly used the newscoms kept for his brother's eventual reading as a booby trap, the papers baled, stacked precariously with barely visible wires here and there that, barely touched, would bring tons of paper cascading.

The stairs were a shambles of paper. A man's legs stuck out from under the bales. The smell came from him.

Wolfe grimaced, held the light between his teeth, lifted two of the bales away. Others threatened to tumble but didn't move.

The man killed by the trap had worn pants, not Davout's customary coveralls, and black boots, badly worn on the edges of the soles.

Wolfe touched the dry, withered skin.

"Dead two, maybe three months," he said softly.

He lifted away more bales, pulled the man free, ready to jump to the side if more papers came down.

He turned the body over, shone his light on the face. He didn't recognize the man.

He went through the man's pockets, found lockpicks, plas cuffs, a folding stiletto, a few bills, an inhaler half full of a brown powder. He opened the vial, sniffed, wrinkled his nose, tossed the drug aside.

He stood, flashed his light up the stairway. Metal, not quite rusted, reflected the light. It was a long jimmy.

He stepped over the burglar's body and started up the stairs.

Davout lived in one long room on the top floor, windows painted black against the light and the world. In the center of the room was the strange mélange of electronics that was Davout's computer, a bastard concoction of mostly military components the man had put together. There was a dim light from four screens, still scrolling endless numbers.

The little man lay on his back beside it, next to his overturned office chair.

Wolfe went to him and shined the light on his face.

Davout's skin was dry, withered. His lips were drawn back in a grin. His eye sockets were black, and something, rats perhaps, had nibbled away most of his ears.

His body showed no signs of violence.

His right hand was clasped over his chest, holding a piece of paper.

Wolfe gently lifted his hand and took the paper.

It was as brown, desiccated, as Davout's skin.

The Federation deeply regrets to inform you that no signs of your brother, Mister Stephen Davout, have been found in any of the worlds retaken thus far. We therefore have determined his status must be considered no longer MISSING but PRESUMED DEAD.

A representative of the government and a trained therapist will be calling on you to assist you in your hour of bereavement, and should you . . .

Wolfe put the years-old com back on Davout's chest, folded both his arms over it, and stood.

"I wondered if he always knew . . ." His voice trailed off.

He put the gun away, turned, went swiftly down the stairs and out of the house.

*

The shattered Al'ar battleship spun in the orbit it had found when the Federation warships left it in its death throes. The system's sun was very dim, very distant.

The killing blast had smashed the drive section of the crescent-shaped warcraft, and most of the crew had died in that moment.

The rest of the Al'ar had been left to their doom. There were blackened sears here and there on the odd reddish-violet metal skin, where destroyers had come close to the fangless monster and blasted away the lifeboat stations.

Wolfe floated out of the *Grayle*'s lock, set his helmet sight on the center of the battleship, touched a stud at his waist. White spray came from his suitjets, and he moved slowly across the half-mile distance toward the ship. He reversed as he approached the Al'ar ship and landed lightly, feet first, near the oval hatch.

Old memories came back, and he found the outer lock controls, pressed them. Nothing happened. Wolfe muttered a curse, took hold of the emergency toggle, and pulled.

Dead machinery came alive, and the hatchway yawned.

He saw the reflection of his face against the faceplate. It was white, drawn. He heard nothing but the rasp of his breathing.

Joshua floated inside.

After a long time, he came out. He pulled behind him an Al'ar deep-space suit and a second garment he had rolled up.

He knelt clumsily, and his lips moved soundlessly.

He pushed himself free of the ship, set his sight once more, triggered the suit drive, returned to the *Grayle*.

He did not look behind him.

*

"I do not understand why I will need a suit, especially not an on-planet outfit on my own world."

"You will. Be silent. I do not wish to have speech with you at this time."

"What is troubling your mind?"

"If you wish to have knowledge," Wolfe said, "it wasn't the happiest day of my life boarding that ship. There were a . . . lot of corpses. Some of them didn't die for a long time after the Federation ships finished with them."

"But why should that bother you?" the Al'ar wondered. **"They are not your people. And dead is dead. Perhaps you are just upset at that Davout friend of yours."**

Wolfe gazed steadily at Taen.

The Al'ar met his gaze. Then Taen's head snapped back, as if he'd been struck.

He rose and left the compartment.

*

The *Grayle* plummeted toward the surface of Sauros, flared less than one hundred feet above the open ground, then settled toward the surface. It stopped about five feet above a flat, metalloid area that had once been used for the Al'ar polygonic "dances." The ship's lock opened.

Bulky packs were tossed out, and two space-suited figures followed them. The lock closed, and the *Grayle* lifted for space.

The two shouldered their packs and ran, stumbling awkwardly, toward a nearby building, careful to follow the winding path.

They disappeared inside.

The echoes of the shipdrive died in the streets of the city, a half-shattered wonderland of multicolored glass, stone, and metal, hues dulled by time and abandon.

No animal moved in the parks, no beings walked the streets.

Two hours later, another noise came, a rhythmic buzzing.

A small winged craft soared down a high corridor of stone, under an arching roadway, through the park, which the Al'ar had called a "reaching-out" place. It orbited the park three times quickly, then another dozen times at its slowest speed, almost stalling.

Its operator reached a decision, and the robot banked and, at full speed, went back down the avenue, echoes of its passing dying as it went.

The two space-suited figures came out, returned to the path, and went through the park, into the city, the taller leading the way.

Neither spoke.

Sometimes the way was clear, sometimes rubble blocked their passage. Storefronts had collapsed, strange goods spilling across the road. But there had been no looting.

They walked for almost half an hour, then stopped in front of a half dome over a smooth ramp that led underground. They went into the cover of the dome and took off their suits.

"You appear to have taken the long way," Wolfe said.

"Not at all," Taen replied. "We could have used the first burrow entrance. But then we would have had to use the civilian ways to reach this military entrance, and I do not know what shape they are in. I wonder that none of your people appears to have landed and collected the spoils of war."

"Some might have," Wolfe said. "But not for long, and it would've been in the first days after the war. The Federation has all the homeworlds under watch now."

"Ah. I did not know that. That is why the drone found me so swiftly when I first came to Sauros. I merely assumed my ship had been detected somewhere in space and followed."

"No. They're scared shitless of whatever's still here. That's why we wore the suits, so their sensors wouldn't pick up any heat or other signs. We'll put them on again when we come back," Wolfe said.

"If we come back this route," the Al'ar added.

"You could also say if we come back at all."

"I could. But I have confidence."

The Al'ar opened his pack, took out what appeared to be a block of white plastic. He unfolded it until it became a thin square about eighteen inches on a side.

He touched a sensor, and the lines of a crudely drawn map appeared.

"The machine we seek, this computer, is one of three used by our Command On High. I learned of it only because the unit I headed that hunted you was assigned directly to them, and I filed my reports here.

"With luck, no one will have discovered it, and our task will be simple," Taen said. "I shall lead. Perhaps my presence will prevent any protective devices from activating."

Wolfe nodded and shouldered his pack.

The two went down the ramp, disappeared from sight.

*

There was a neat hole in one corridor wall and, on the other side, a gaping, jagged opening.

"I do not like this," Taen said. "Someone who did not know the code came this way and triggered the weapon."

Wolfe knelt, touched the deck, and *felt* around him. The Lumina in its hidden pouch warmed to his touch. He rose.

"Someone . . . maybe two, three people died when they set off this trap."

"Terrans?"

Wolfe nodded.

"Yet there is no sign of a body. Still worse," Taen said.

"Renegades don't worry about corpses," Joshua agreed. "These people would've been part of some organization."

They went up a winding, curved corridor. The Al'ar abominated straight lines in length, so their buildings turned, swept, as did their roads and tunnels.

Wolfe had to stop three times to reorient himself as they went.

They went on another half mile. Twice Taen touched a blank section of wall, then told Wolfe it was safe to proceed.

The corridor ended abruptly. Taen stood in a certain place, took two steps at the side, and the wall lifted, revealing a high, rounded chamber. But no lights came on, and Wolfe smelled the old stink of seared flesh, ozone, *felt* fear and agony.

There were control panels ranked around the walls, but blaster bolts had torn and ripped them.

Taen made a soft noise of pain.

Once more Wolfe *felt* around him.

"Men were killed here," he said softly. "There aren't any bodies, so this must've been a Federation Intelligence group, not renegade looters. Probably one of our Analysis teams. Scientists, engineers, mostly. I guess they found this, tried to operate it."

"And the machine killed them," Taen said.

"Killing itself in the process."

"No," the Al'ar said. "This is but an operating station. The computer itself is safe far away, far below us. But what upsets me is that I was wrong. I told you that the computer itself would have no safeguards. I was wrong. I wonder what else I am wrong about.

"We must seek one of the secondary stations. I know the approximate location of one."

*

They stopped twice, ate rations from their packs that Wolfe hardly tasted, stopped a third time, slept briefly.

Wolfe woke with the memory of buzzing, felt the burns on his arm.

*

The man sprawled on his back, a look of mild surprise still visible. His build was slight, thin, and the face was that of a scientist, a thinker. His cheeks had begun to pull back into a rictus.

There was a hole where his chest had been and a pile of white dust above and below the hole where a strange decay was spreading.

"This was a looter," Wolfe said. "Somebody managed to land without alerting the Federation or else came down before the interdiction was put on."

"What would he have sought?"

"Hardware. Programming. Raw knowledge, maybe. The word was your computers were faster, more intuitive than ours. I never knew anybody who'd operated both, so I can't say. He must've believed the story. He"—Wolfe looked around at the other six bodies—"and his friends. They had enough brains to find this place . . ." He shrugged. "Now what do we do?"

"I do not like this at all," the Al'ar said.

"I'm not exactly overjoyed. What are our options? Find another world?"

"No. This is the only location I know for certain. We

could spend the rest of our lives on other homeworlds' undergrounds, looking," Taen said.

"And maybe running into another one of these nasty little traps," Wolfe said. "All right. We'll come up with another plan that doesn't require heavy thinking. Drop the computer idea."

"We have one option. We could seek out the computer itself."

"Which you said is under us. How far down did the Al'ar dig? I never knew of anything other than the upper civilian levels when I lived here, you know."

"We dug . . . very deeply."

"You said we could spend two forevers looking for a simple operating station. How will it be easier looking for Big Mama?"

"Easier in the looking because its location will be close to our Final Command Station. This is where we would have fought from, if you had landed on Sauros. Instead . . . we found another Way."

"All right. And I would guess that there'll be even more traps for intruders."

"Not just for Terrans," Taen said. "No Al'ar was permitted to go to these places without special permission, guides, and passes." He paused. "The machine will be as perfect a deathtrap as our finest soldiers could devise."

* **CHAPTER SEVEN** *

The ramps curled down into darkness, broken now and again as still-sensing lamps flared, died as they passed.

Three levels below the military tunnel system, huge doors hung open. Inside was a great hangar with lines of in-atmosphere interceptors, sagging drunkenly, their skid-shocks slowly collapsing as fluid leaked away.

"We would have launched these when your ships entered Sauros' atmosphere," Taen explained. **"Buildings above had been constructed with demolition charges so they would fall away at the proper time."**

"Clever," Wolfe said neutrally. Both spoke in Al'ar. It seemed safer.

The next level was barracks for the pilots and maintenance crews, with long rows of resting racks stretching away into darkness. The padding on the racks had begun to unravel and trailed on the decks. Wolfe noted that nothing, not man, not rat, not cat, had made trails in the thick dust. He thought he could hear the faint whisper of a still-functioning air-circulation system.

Taen moved in front of Joshua as they went on. Wolfe found his hand hovering over his gun and grinned wryly, wondering what in this long-dead labyrinth would need shooting. Booby traps are impervious to a quick draw.

Taen held up a grasping organ, crouched, and pointed to the wall. Wolfe saw nothing, *felt* beyond.

Death . . . the snout of a blaster muzzle behind the met-alloid . . . trigger-sensor still alive . . .

They crawled under the sensor, got up, and went on.

The corridor they were in opened up, the walls hidden in the gloom, and another ramp went down, winding, turning. Joshua *felt* great space around him.

More and more of the automatic lights had failed, and so they took flashes from their packs, continued on.

Wolfe heard a whine of gears and went flat. The sound grew louder, and the ramp swiveled sideways, trying to dump them off. Joshua scrabbled toward the edge of the ramp as it turned, held it, and Taen's grasping organs had him by the leg.

He hung, gasping, over emptiness.

The Al'ar clawed his way up Wolfe's body, found a hold on the ramp, and they clung for long moments until the ramp settled back to level.

"I did not sense that coming," Taen whispered.

"Nor I. I heard the sound of its machinery just before it began functioning."

"But you sensed it before I. Perhaps you should lead. I must tell you that none of these devices was operative the times I was ordered to come this way."

Wolfe hesitated, then obeyed. The Lumina was warm against his skin. The darkness around him was chill and smelled faintly of ozone.

The walls drew in once more, and they walked down a corridor that might have been on a spaceship.

At the end of the passage was a door. Wolfe was about to insert a finger into the opening sensor notch, then stopped. He knelt, peered into the slot, saw nothing.

He took the pack from his back, and pulled out a jimmy and a hammer. He motioned Taen out of the way, then tapped the dogs of the hinge free, caught the door as it tottered, and eased it to the deck.

Taen held up his grasping organs in a questioning gesture. Wolfe turned the door over and slid the tip of the jimmy into the sensor notch, turning his head away as he did.

A violet laser-blast flashed, burning a half-inch hole in the ceiling above them. Taen hissed, said nothing.

Their way was level once more. Taen came close, whispered, **"Now we are on the base level. What we seek should be close."**

Once more the walls were far distant, invisible. Wolfe coughed, and sound echoed into the distance.

Taen took the lead again and went on, his head moving back and forth like a questing hound's.

Domes, some small, some huge, rose around them. Taen stopped at one.

"Here is the place we would have commanded the final battle from."

Curious, Wolfe started to activate the door to the command center. Taen stopped him.

"Our business is not in there. Why should we risk encountering another trap?"

Wolfe held up his hands, agreeing, and abandoned curiosity.

He heard the purring of engines and then light crashed up around them, blinding them. The engine-sound grew louder, and something hovered toward them from the darkness.

Wolfe knew it from the war.

It was a four-barreled auto-cannon, triggers linked to motion detectors. Wolfe rolled as the cannon churned rounds, tearing up the metal deck where he'd been. The cannon swiveled, long-disused bearings squealing, spat a stream of solid bullets, and once more he rolled, coming up in a squat.

The Lumina burned against him as he frog-jumped sideways, and the cannon swept past him.

He froze, barely breathing. The cannon's pickups scanned the area he was in, found nothing, swept in increasingly greater arcs.

Wolfe inhaled sharply, about to dive for the gun's base, into its dead zone, and Taen rose from the darkness, blaster in both grasping organs, and blew the sensor off the cannon-mount.

The cannon blatted a burst into nowhere, ground into silence. It floated away, aimlessly, its guns looking here, there, nowhere.

Taen beckoned, and Wolfe followed him, around the great bulk of the command center.

An arched doorway rose from the deck. Taen tried the opening sensor. The door remained locked.

Wolfe took lockpicks from his beltpouch and slipped them into the slot. He *felt* as he moved them, trying to think as an Al'ar.

He felt a humming through the picks, jerked his hands out as the door slid smoothly open.

Inside were the banks of a great Al'ar strategy computer.

*

Taen slid his hand down a multicolored strip next to a rack, and around him screens lit. A larger screen, almost a yard on a side just in front of Taen remained blue-black, inactive.

"It lives!"

"It would have been a not life-enhancing experience if it had not, considering our passage," Wolfe said.

"That is what you call sarcasm **I would guess,"** Taen said. **"I did not know it was possible to do that in Al'ar."**

The holograph rose in front of him, the computer's "keyboard." Dim green light formed vertical squares, and in each was a character or combination of characters in Al'ar.

"Let us hope that it will recognize me."

Wolfe pulled up a resting rack and made himself as comfortable as possible.

Two hours later the dark screen in front of Taen blinked into life, swirled through a color wheel, shades unseen by Wolfe since he was last on an Al'ar world.

"Now we have a starting point," Taen said.

"Start by asking about the Guardians."

Taen's impossibly long fingers moved, screens showed figures, then a diagonal multicolored band appeared across the main screen. Taen's grasping organ shot out, and the screen blanked.

"That I do not like."

"What occurred?" Wolfe asked.

"Be silent. Let me attempt the task again."

Again his fingers moved against the "keyboard," and again the diagonal band flashed and Taen was cut out of the program.

"The machine has defenses and takes precautions. I thought I had a high-enough permission, what you call clearance, but any attempt to inquire in the area of Guardians produces a warning. If I persisted, I suspect the whole computer would shut down on me. Do you have a suggestion?"

"I think," Wolfe said, "we stay light-years away from that area. You realize that what just happened confirms the existence of the Guardians."

Taen's hood flared slightly, then subsided. "No, I had not yet . . . of course. Certainly it must. I wonder what has become of my intelligence? I am behaving entirely like a broodling."

"Don't concern yourself," Wolfe said. "I never thought you were highly gifted in the arena of thinking."

"Such is obvious," Taen said. "I chose to associate with Terrans."

Wolfe looked at the Al'ar in considerable astonishment. "Taen, did you just make a joke?" he asked in Terran.

"Perhaps I did. It was an error. How shall we pursue the matter now?"

"I wondered if there might not be some kind of block within the computer," Wolfe said, "so I brought some backup." He dug in his pack and took out two microfiches, a viewer, and a notepad.

"This will take a few minutes," he said, inserting the card into the viewer's slot. "If we can't get 'em high, perhaps we can nail them down low."

*

"What are these locations?"

"These are twelve battles fought during the war. I got them from the standard Federation history of the Al'ar war. We gave these battles their own names, which I assume could have different labels in Al'ar, so what you're looking at are just the ana/kata coordinates."

"Why were—are these battles special?"

"Because these were fought in the middle of nowhere, for no discernible reason. All of them are deep inside the Al'ar sectors. Generally a Federation Fleet or Fleets would be traversing a certain area and be met with a sudden attack that ended only with the complete defeat of one or another force."

"What makes that extraordinary? There were many such fights."

"True. But these catfights appear to have been by accident, and especially ferocious, when our forces stumbled into yours. The Al'ar ships were already in place, as if they were holding a specific defensive position."

"Perhaps," Taen said, "your security was inadequate. Perhaps our forces had advance knowledge of your Fleet movements and were able to prepare ambushes."

"That was what the Federation Command worried about. I was consulted on two of the battles, which is why I remembered them. They'd assembled all data on the two events, but no one could find any congruence that might suggest a mole. They wanted to know if I could provide any interpretation of what happened. I failed. The explanation settled on was the imbecilic one of 'aliens do alien things in an alien way.' "

"Do not be angry at them. My own Command On

High frequently used the same simplistic thinking," Taen said.

Wolfe returned to Al'ar. "I would like you to examine these locations on a small-scale starchart and tell me what the computer tells you about them."

"I do not understand what you are seeking, but I shall obey. Rest yourself. This shall take some time, even with a device as sophisticated as this."

*

"I have some interesting data," Taen announced. "First, I can confirm your hypothesis that these battles were anomalous, being fought far distant from any known Al'ar bases and not part of any known offensive plan. Look at these two. Nearly in the same location, yet fought seven years apart.

"What could have been so valuable about that sector of seemingly empty space that our forces would defend it so resolutely, as well as all the others?"

Wolfe's eyes gleamed. "I can conjecture a better place to begin thinking," he said. "Take those two points and connect them. Project the line out."

"I have done this."

"Now take the other battles, and project a line from each of them to intersect with this line."

"Shadow Warrior," Taen said, and Wolfe thought he detected impossible emotion in his voice, "the intersection point is at the fringes of our sectors, but well within the area of Al'ar control."

"Worthy of consideration," Wolfe said. "Now, might you not wonder if our Fleets just happened to wander into these areas and were brought to battle because they were on the 'approaches' to something very secret, something that perhaps even the forces assigned to defend them might not be informed of?"

"Such as the planet of the Guardians?" the Al'ar said. "You do not have enough data to make such an inference."

"Here might be an additional piece of data. Can you find out what units were involved in any of these battles?"

"Perhaps." Taen's fingers blurred once more. Time passed.

"Unusual," he said finally. "I can find an order of battle for five of the earlier conflicts, but nothing on the later ones."

"I find it significant," Wolfe said, "that all records of units can be blanked from the files of a strategy computer. This is generally done only when a formation is involved in something most secret. Such as defending the Guardians.

"Try to find out anything about any of those units, what we call the unit history, which is kept from day to day."

"Our military also had the custom. I shall try."

Wolfe watched as Taen again manipulated the machine. Quite suddenly a diagonal bar slashed across the main screen, and Taen blanked away from his search.

"The same cutout for security reasons as when we inquired about the Guardians?" Wolfe asked.

"Just so," Taen said.

"Will you allow that as a second, possibly confirmatory bit of data?"

"I shall."

"Might it not be interesting to return to our ship

and make periodic jumps down that line, toward that point, to see what we might encounter?"

Taen turned from the "keyboard." His hood was fully flared. "You might have found the path, Joshua Wolfe. I hope your thinking bears fruit."

"Me, too. But let's look up something else, as long as we're up to our elbows in Al'ar secrets."

*

"I cannot believe your Command On High placed such a low secrecy value on this file."

"Why should they have?" Taen said. "Now you are thinking like a Terran, not like an Al'ar.

"This information needed no higher a classification than to prevent the casual reader from seeing it. Otherwise, it offered what our leaders thought was a valuable insight into the dishonorable nature of the enemy, something any battle commander might find valuable."

"I am sorry," Wolfe said. "I stand corrected. But this is in an older form of your language. I have trouble reading it. Would you give me its merits briefly?"

"I shall. This is the summary of what occurred when a group of Terrans who called themselves Chitet secretly visited our civilization, about two hundred Earth-years ago.

"They felt that they were predestined to rule the Universe and wished to form an alliance with the Al'ar to share this power with them."

"Did the Al'ar know the Chitet had attempted a coup against the Federation about a hundred years before that?"

"They were informed of this by the leader of the expedition. They spent much time discussing the situation with the Chitet and were somewhat bewildered at just what secret powers my race was supposed to possess beyond the obvious, the known.

"These Chitet were equally vague about just what they sought, but said that their projections of future history showed, once the unexpected appearance of the Al'ar was integrated, that nothing in their projection would be altered. Their role as Rulers-to-Be was still a given."

"What," Wolfe said in Terran, "was the response to that? Why didn't your leaders accept their offer? They could always have double-crossed them later. The Al'ar," he said dryly, "weren't exactly bound by human standards of fair play."

"The offer was not accepted, according to this file, for two reasons. The first was that our leaders had not finally determined that war between our races was inevitable. Perhaps that was foolish of them. The second reason is that all traitors are always unreliable. A blade that slips once in the hand and cuts its wielder will most likely turn once more."

"True. What happened then?"

"The head of the Chitet expedition evinced the Terran emotion called anger, and said if the Al'ar did not change their minds, when the Chitet returned to the Federation they would announce they had discovered secret battle plans for the obliteration of humanity. It is sad, but of course no such plans existed at that time."

"Now that," Wolfe said, "was one of the dumbest-assed things I've ever heard of. Sit in the middle of the enemy and try blackmail. So that was why all seven of the ships were destroyed and their crews slotted. And these clowns call themselves the most logical folks who ever lived." He snorted amusement.

"Of course," the Al'ar said. **"I will make a side comment here. How can these Chitet be logical, if they, and I use your words, call themselves *most* logical?**

"Logic is a condition, an absolute. Can a Terran be a little bit alive? A little bit dead?"

"You've never been to some of the bars I have on a Sunday night," Wolfe said in Terran. He switched back to Al'ar. **"So all these years this must have been working at the Chitet. They valued the war, because they imagined that when it was won by the Terrans, they would be able to find this secret weapon, or whatever it was. And now they're trying once more. What in the—what can they be seeking?"**

"Perhaps we should seek them out and ask them."

"Perhaps so." Wolfe looked thoughtful. **"But we've got a line to follow first."**

* CHAPTER EIGHT *

The *Grayle* banked into the street and hovered as her port slid open. Taen and Wolfe doubled from the shelter of the subway entrance to the ramp and went up it, and the ship climbed away.

"I was observed entering atmosphere," the ship reported. *"A robot craft was launched to investigate, according to my sensors."*

"Well, shame on you for getting sloppy. Will the bird, sorry, the craft come within observation range?"

"Negative."

"Then don't worry about it. Ship, when clear of atmosphere, assume the electronic characteristics of a *Sorge*-type vessel. I remember that as being in your repertoire. Let's give the Federation patrollers some confusion if they pick us up."

"Understood. Request name."

"I guess it'd be subverting the purpose of a spyship to call yourself the *Philby*. Umm, you're now the *Harnack*. I don't think anyone will catch that."

"Understood."

"As soon as we're able, blindjump us away from Sauros. You will be given the coordinates."

"Understood."

Wolfe stretched hugely. "Taen, I want a shower, about two pounds of near-raw animal tissue, a decent glass of fermented grape juice, and ten straight hours of sleep. And I'll kill anyone who gets between me and them."

The ship answered: *"My sensors report a ship within range. It has not yet detected us but will within seconds. I shall not be able to evade detection."*

"I made a promise," Wolfe said. "I'll keep it. Open all frequencies. Let's see who I'm going to murder."

Five minutes later the call came: "Unknown ship, unknown ship. Please cut your drive, and stand by for boarding and inspection."

"Son of a bitch," Wolfe swore. "The singer's a little more polite, but I still don't like the song."

"The Chitet," Taen said.

"Yeah. I guess they're running their own interdiction out here, as well as the Federation Navy. How many goddamned ships do they have, anyway? Ship, what are the characteristics of the craft?"

"I would identify the ship in question as being a light corvette, Federation-built, Hamilton *class. It has superior armament, but its performance capabilities when new were inferior to mine."*

"Finally," Wolfe said. "Something we can just run away from."

"Perhaps," Taen said, "that may not be the best idea?"

Wolfe looked skeptically at the Al'ar. "You will have to do some serious convincement to make me believe we should stand and fight a *Hamilton*-class corvette."

"I think we can devise a strategy for that."

"So what's the purpose, besides general piss-off at being chased around so much?"

"In battle," Taen said carefully, **"sometimes a war leader can be distracted by the unexpected. Especially when it is aimed at himself and comes from nowhere."**

"Hmm." Wolfe considered.

"The corvette is broadcasting once more, with the same message," the *Grayle* said. "What should my reply be?"

"Stand by," Wolfe said. "All right. Let's start the ball rolling with your scheme. You can explain as we go."

*

"Unknown ship, unknown ship, cut your drive immediately. We are armed, and will launch missiles unless you obey our command instantly. This is your last warning."

"Now, this one I'm particularly proud of," Wolfe said. "Built her all by myself. Watch the third screen."

He touched sensors, swung a mike down, touched other sensors. One screen showed the computer simulation of the approaching Chitet spacecraft.

The screen Wolfe had told Taen to watch cleared, and the image of a rather handsome woman appeared, wearing a Federation Naval uniform.

"This is the Federation Monitor ship *Harnack*," Wolfe said, and the onscreen lips moved. "Who is attempting to contact this unit?"

Static blared, then:

"This . . . this is the exploration ship *Occam*," the voice said, now sounding unsure of itself. "We are conducting an authorized control of the space around the planet Sauros. We request we be permitted to board and inspect your vessel."

Wolfe touched sensors, and the woman onscreen frowned in anger.

"I say again, this is the Federation naval vessel *Harnack*. How dare you order a Federation ship to do anything?"

"Please stand by," the voice bleated. "I am summoning the captain."

"Occam, eh? Another goddamned logician." Wolfe grinned tightly, waited.

"This is Captain Millet of the *Occam*. My watch officer reports that you are a Federation naval vessel. Is that correct?"

"Affirm."

"Would you please transmit your recognition signal?"

"We do not have such data," Taen said.

"Neither do they. Spoofing people who want codes is easier than standing on your head in a zip-gee field. Ship, broadcast blue, green, blue-white colorbands."

"Understood. Transmission complete."

There was dead air for a time, then:

"*Harnack*, this is *Occam*. I do not understand your signal. That is not on the list of recognition signals we were provided."

"*Occam*, this is Captain Dailey of the *Harnack*. I am thoroughly tired of this nonsense. By what right do you have to order any ship to stop anywhere at any time?"

"I have my orders from my superiors." Now Millet's voice was as uncertain as his subordinate's. "It is my understanding that such a matter has already been arranged between our governments."

"This is *Harnack*." The woman appeared completely outraged. "Perhaps you are not aware of the function of a monitoring vessel. We operate directly under Federation High Command on matters of the most critical importance. I received no such information from my own superiors before undertaking my mission and doubt whether any such understanding exists.

"Now, sir, I have orders for you. You will cut your drive and stand by. I have already sent a com reporting this absurd incident. I propose to board you and examine your papers. Any attempts to resist will be met with the appropriate response. Do you understand, sir?"

A long silence, then:

"Message understood. We are obeying your instructions." Then, plaintively: "I am sure this matter will be settled to our mutual satisfaction."

Again Wolfe smiled, a smile that was not at all humorous.

*

The watch officer waited nervously in the port. Beside him two other Chitet stood, hastily adjusting their best shipsuits.

He felt a hum of a shipdrive as the other ship closed with his, the clang as their ports met, sealed.

He stiffened to attention, determined to impress this martinet of a Federation captain before she could do his career any further damage.

The port opened, and utter horror burst out, impossibly thin and corpse-white, a nightmare that should no longer exist. The officer clawed for his pistol, fell dead with half his face blown away.

As the corpse fell, one of the other Chitet was killed

where he stood; the second managed two steps and a gargling scream before he, too, died.

The *Occam*'s intercom chattered something as Wolfe cleared the lock. He wore a light Federation naval spacesuit, carried a pistol in one hand, a fighting knife in the other.

"That way," he said, voice metallic through the suit's external speaker. "To the bridge."

A man looked around the port and ducked back as Wolfe fired, searing a hole in the bulkhead where he'd been. Joshua jumped to the passageway, sent three blaster bolts down it without looking, and ran in the direction he'd indicated.

*

There were five humans in quiet, plain-colored shipsuits on the bridge of the *Occam*. Four of them were still alive. The fifth lay sprawled across a nav table, blood from his slashed throat pooling on a starchart. The four had their hands in the air.

"Come on, Millet," Wolfe shouted. "Tell them, or I blow the atmosphere unit."

The captain hesitated, then keyed a mike. "All hands, all hands, this is the skipper. We have been attacked, and I have surrendered the ship. Do not offer any resistance. I repeat, do not offer any resistance."

He looked at Wolfe, features invisible in the darkened faceplate. "What do I do next?"

"All hands to Supply Hold Delta," Wolfe said. "Five minutes. If anybody shoots, we dump the air. Five minutes, we dump the air anyway."

"But—what does the Federation—why—how can—" one of the other men on the bridge sputtered.

Wolfe sent a bolt shattering past his face in reply, and two screens on the control board fragmented. The man yelped and ducked.

"No questions, no goddamn answers! Let's go, let's go, let's go!" Wolfe shouted, herding them toward the compartment hatchway.

They moved, stumbling, not looking where they were going, eyes returning again and again to the impossible form of the Al'ar, standing silent, gun ready.

*

"So what did you do with the crew?" Cormac asked.

"We dumped them on . . . let's say a certain world where they'll be able to reach civilization in a week, maybe two. They had plenty of rations, two guns."

"You're getting soft in your old age, Ghost Actual," Cormac said. "I can remember a time when—"

"That's what . . . someone else accused me of," Wolfe interrupted. "Guess that's the price of being lovable. Besides, they saw—or think they saw—some things I'd like people to learn about in a while. I'm trying to complicate some lives with this one."

Cormac snickered, turned serious. "Always wheels within wheels. Anyway, I can rig the ship the way you want it. I guess you'll want me to do it myself, right?"

"By preference. The only way three people can keep a secret is if two of them're dead."

"All right," Cormac said. "You haven't gotten that lovable. Just as a guesstimate, I suppose you want me to rig you up a deepspace HAHO rig as well?"

"Just like the old days."

"Except with different enemies."

Wolfe shrugged. "I never could tell the difference between folks who were trying to kill me. By the way. I need this stuff yesterday, and I mean yesterday."

"Of course. Like always. You know, I could drag things out," the shiprigger said. "Make sure you're around for the wedding. I could use a best man."

"You're getting married?"

"Yeah." Cormac looked sheepish. "I'm old-fashioned."

"Not this time," Wolfe said, real regret in his voice. "I'm moving too fast to touch down."

Cormac spread his hands. "I tried."

*

The *Grayle* and the *Occam*, slaved together, lifted away from Malabar, reached their first jump point, disappeared.

*

"Countdown to fifth jump," the ship announced.

Wolfe put the book down on his chest and waited.

Time, space moved around him, and the *Grayle* came out of N-space. His eyes returned to the book, read two paragraphs, then he tossed the volume, *An Examination of the Relationship Among Ezra Pound, the Provençal Poets, and the Cygnus XII School of the Early 27th Century*, in the general direction of the overflowing bookcase. It thudded down, the magnet in its spine holding it in place.

"Now that," he said softly, "is easily the dullest goddamn book I've tried to read in ten years." He went down the passage and rapped at the door to Taen's compartment.

"Come on, you alien monster. Let's see if you can break a few more of my bones."

*

"So now we are in the heart of the Federation. Probably farther than any other Al'ar not on a diplomatic mission ever achieved," Taen said.

"We are. And you'll be thrilled to note this section of space is wildly different, far more colorful and exciting than any other we have transited."

"Sarcasm **once more**."

"When I was a boy," Wolfe said, "I couldn't wait until I made my first jump. Things were very glamorous in the romances, with ships hurtling past comets and planets and suns. I guess I thought it was like being on a bullet train at night, when you could look out and see the lights of the cities flash past. Then I found out that all you see is computer simulations unless you're too damned close, and there's nothing at all in N-space. More like the first time I rode the sea-train from Calais to New York, except there wasn't even the ocean to stare at."

"**All hatchlings imagine things to be different than they are.**"

"Did I ever say that reminiscing with you is just about as much fun as watching rocks become sand?"

*

"This is the starship *Normandie* to unknown paired ships. Please respond."

Wolfe, looking worried, swung the mike down. "*Normandie*, this is the tug *Foss Enterprise*. Go ahead."

"This is the *Normandie*, First Officer Wu. Is that a *Hamilton*-class corvette you're pulling?"

"*Normandie*, this is the *Foss Enterprise*. That's affirmative. It's the mothballed *Hailsworth*."

"I thought I recognized my screen projection, *Foss Enterprise*," the woman's voice said. "I was just curious.

I commanded the *Hetty Green* during the war. I don't think I want to ask, but where're you taking her to?"

"You're right. You didn't want to know. She's headed for the knackers' yard."

A sound very much like a sigh came from the speaker. "Thanks, *Foss Enterprise*. What's the line . . . 'but at my back/I always hear/Time's winged chariot,' something or other?"

"That's 'hurrying near,' *Normandie*."

"Yeah. That's it. This is the *Normandie*, out."

Wolfe turned away the speaker. "Nice to see there's at least one other sentimental slob out here."

"I do not like this," Taen replied. **"That was the fourth ship onscreen within the past few ship-hours. There are too many starships in this sector. There is too much chance of our being detected and challenged by either a Chitet ship or Federation Navy."**

"Now you're the one who's not thinking right," Wolfe said. "Here, inside the Federation, there's no reason for any naval vessel to challenge a ship proceeding on lawful business, and sure as hell no Chitet would dream of doing that. Hide in plain sight, and all that."

"You are correct. I was thinking like an Al'ar, like an enemy."

*

"This will be the last jump. Estimated distance from target world of Batan three ship-days' journey if all nav-aids correct," the ship said.

The world twisted, changed, and the *Grayle* entered normal space.

Half filling the screen in front of them was the capital world of the Chitet.

*

By his conservative dress, the man onscreen might have been a preacher. He was not.

With further good news for our people, Master Speaker Athelstan announced a two percent reduction in the approved luxury tax. This, he said, was due to the excellent and mature response from us all when he announced last ten-month that we were consuming all too many nonessential goods and services. He promised that if this reasoned pattern continues, it might be possible . . .

Joshua turned away from the measured movements of the newscaster's face.

"Nice to hear that," he said. "It'd be a real pain if the bastard wasn't home to give us a nice, logical response to events."

*

"It has been too long since I've done stupid things like this," Joshua said.

He wore a bulky deepspace suit and stood next to a stack of metal rafts nearly as tall as he was, Cormac's High Altitude, High Opening rig. Short lengths of chain ran to rigid metal bars connected to the four corners of the bottom raft. The small hold of the *Grayle* was crowded.

"Twelve beat until the correct time," Taen said. He sealed his own suit.

Joshua snapped his faceplate shut. "Any time."

"Atmosphere being removed."

The slight ambient noise coming through the suit's insulation died.

The air rushing out into space tugged at the Al'ar, and he steadied himself against a stanchion.

The lock opened all the way, and Joshua stared out at the green-and-white bulk of Batan. They were only a few hundred miles above the planet, barely outside range of the Landing Authority.

Taen and Joshua slid the metal stack to the edge of the hold, and Joshua floated out into space.

The chains grew taut and pulled him gently away from the *Grayle*. The lock door closed.

He spoke into the bonemike. *"Execute orbital change as directed. You now are required to take commands from either this station or from the one who remains aboard."*

"Understood."

Joshua saw brief wisps from the ship's secondary drive, and slowly the two starships moved away from him.

"Orient suit. On zero," the ship said, *"fire suit drive . . . five . . . four . . . three . . . two . . . fire."*

Wolfe had turned as the *Grayle* instructed him and, on count, twisted the red handle on the canister attached to his stomach. Gas hissed for a time, then the cylinder was empty. He pulled two D-rings and let the container float away to find its own orbit as he began his descent into gravity.

He hung in a world of black and light, the small dots of stars moving around him while the great mass of Batan drew closer.

*

Wolfe ate twice, slept once while he closed on Batan. He woke, stretched within the confines of the suit, and sucked refreshment from the nipple beside the faceplate.

He blanked the faceplate and ran through the suit's entertainment suite, found nothing suitable and reopened the window on his womb.

He stared at the cold dead stars beyond, couldn't spot the *Grayle*, let the suit turn slowly until Batan was all that could be seen.

He watched the world turn, saw clouds spin, unwind, crawl over the planet's curve, and realized, dimly, that he was quite happy.

*

The programmed proximity detector brought him back from a dream he could not quite remember.

"In-exosphere," the voice buzzed. *"Distance to ground, eight hundred miles."*

Time passed. Again he ate, drank, voided into the suit's disposal compartments, dumped them, looked at his waste distastefully, then tucked into a vee and moved away from the debris.

"External temperature rising," the suit sensor told him. *"Suggest deployment first generator within five minutes."*

Wolfe thought he could feel atmosphere rush and turned on an outside microphone, heard noise as he hurtled down toward green and blue.

Four minutes later, he touched another sensor, and the first of the antigrav generators rafted above him released its catches, deployed to the length of its twenty-foot chain, and turned itself on slowly.

Wolfe felt gravity drag, and he was pulled upright by the chains linked to the shoulders of his suit.

He rode the generator for fifty miles while Batan stabilized under him, turning until it was still night below, then cut the generator away and free-fell until he saw the suit's metal turning a flecked heat-gray.

Three more times, as he fell deeper into the planet's atmosphere, he activated, then cut away the antigravity "rafts" above.

He rode the last-but-one generator to ten miles above the surface, then cut loose from that.

Wolfe touched a key, and the tiny screens above his faceplate dropped down and showed him where he was in relation to his target. He decided he was a little long and to the east, but his position was acceptable. He retracted the screens and looked down.

It was about two hours before dawn in the city below, well within his desired arrival time.

He saw the mountain the city had been built against and deployed the last generator.

He grunted when it went on, feeling the jerk. "Waited a little long," he murmured, and dialed the power up until he hung motionless in the sky.

The dawn wind carried him behind the mountain, gave it to him for a shield. The wind eddied around the peak, back toward the city. Wolfe reduced power and bled off altitude.

Now he was in the first swell of daylight.

He looked below and saw the sun's rays touch a great palace's dark-gray stones. The spires were squared, tapering slightly to blunt tips, imagination constrained, dreams allowed but within limits.

The lake that was his target was just below. He thought the breeze was carrying him too close to the shore, chopped his power, and free-fell the last thirty feet to splash into the water.

He grimaced, muttered something about getting sloppy and out of practice, and let himself sink to the lake's bottom, some seventy feet down. He sunk to about midthigh in muck. The generator thudded against his helmet and slipped off into the mire beside him.

Wolfe unfastened the chains that held him to the generator, turned on the suit's integral antigrav generator until he nearly lifted clear of the mud, then began wading toward shore, following the compass direction illuminated above his faceplate.

It was slow, laborious going, but he was in no hurry.

After two hours, he turned on an exterior camera, swiveled it to look up, and saw the silver plate of the surface about fifteen feet above. He turned the antigrav off, settled down to wait.

Several times curious fish floated around, one an orange extravagance with long, white fins and an expression of incredible stupidity. Once the camera blipped alert, and he saw the oval of a boat move above him. At last the suit clock told him it was night again, and he turned the suit's antigrav on and went toward the land.

*

The boy and the girl sitting on the grass verge of the lake did not appear to be behaving in a calm, logical, Chitet manner.

She broke away from his embrace, slid the fastener of her soberly green tunic open, tossed it away.

The boy embraced her, and they lay back on the grass.

A few minutes later, she lifted her hips, wriggled out of her slacks. Her legs came up, curled around the back of his thighs as he moved over her.

Neither of them could have seen the metallic dome that broke the surface, rose, then submerged again.

Joshua surfaced once more around the curve of a small point, saw no one on the land, and waded ashore, a dark alloy gorilla in the night.

He went as quickly as he could into the trees, found one with a considerable overhang, ducked underneath the branches, and sat.

He unsealed his faceplate, drank in air that smelled like something other than sterility and Joshua Wolfe.

There were two moons overhead, one, slightly pinkish, racing past like an aircraft, the other, mottled orange, hanging motionless, half full, above and to one side of the residence of the Master Speaker.

There were many lights in the palace, and Wolfe supposed the Chitet leader was entertaining. He wondered briefly what their idea of entertainment would be, then decided that a rousing debate on whether Srinivasi Ramanujan would have been greater than Einstein if he'd lived was about the height of their decadence.

He unclipped the magclips of his pack, opened it, and took out a transceiver with an archaic key instead of a microphone.

The other device in the pack looked like a rather bulky small telescope, with a tripod. He extended and opened the legs, and set it in front of him. He peered through the eyepiece, focused it on the palace's central tower, locked the elevating wheels down.

Then he turned the transceiver on, swung the key out, and tapped K, K, K, K, waited.

The old dot/dash code came back from the *Grayle* in orbit off Batan: $R \ldots R \ldots R \ldots$

When he heard the first letter, he turned a timer in his suit on.

He touched a stud on the scope, looked again through the eyepiece. Now the tower appeared to be lit by a strange, reddish glow.

Joshua moved back from the apparatus, careful not to disturb anything, and sent X ... X ... X ... X ...

The timer showed forty-seven seconds when he thought he saw something high above the palace, then heard the whine of the *Occam*'s secondary drive.

There might have been raving madness in the Landing Authority's control rooms and in Batan's aerial defense network. Wolfe heard, saw nothing except the ship plunging down, homing on the laser beam painting the tower.

It struck, and the palace exploded in a red-and-gray ruin, flames gouting high into the sky. Wolfe thought he saw the ruins of the *Occam* pinwheeling away to smash down in a courtyard but wasn't sure.

He sent Z ... Z ... Z ... Z on the transceiver, then stowed it and the illuminator in the pack and set the melt-down timer to thirty seconds. He pushed his way out of the overhang and hurled the pack out into the lake. It sank rapidly. He barely saw the white flare as the detonator went off underwater.

"Federation pirates taking Chitet ships ... an Al'ar on board ... a suicide attack on Athelstan with one of his own craft," he murmured. "Yeah, Taen. I guess we have distracted them a little bit. Now we can go for the main chance."

He looked again at the palace as explosions rocked the ground, almost knocking him down, then waddled away, waiting for the *Grayle* to home on his suit's signal.

* CHAPTER NINE *

Death Strikes At Chitet Master
Suicide Ship Smashes Palace,
Athelstan Safe

Press for More

BATAN—Unknown attackers sent a starship crashing into the Residence of Chitet Master Speaker Matteos Athelstan.

Athelstan was slightly burned and concussed in the attack, but otherwise uninjured. At least 50 high-ranking Chitet officials and a greater number of his Residency staff were killed and more than four times that number injured when the starship slammed into the historic palace shortly after midnight, local time, this date.

A Residency spokesperson said that an important conference, the subject of which is secret, was being held, which accounted for the great number of government officials present at that late an hour.

The Residency, completed less than a year ago and first occupied by Speaker Athelstan, was regarded as a physical embodiment of the group, which now claims several billion adherents on over 100 worlds.

The Chitet's highest-ranking Authority Coordinator, Dina Kur, said no conceivable motive for the murderous attack is known, nor has any terrorist group claimed responsibility. The ownership of the starship and the type of ship are under investigation.

"Obviously," Coordinator Kur said, "the disturbed ones responsible for this outrage shall be brought to the bar, either by our own representatives of order or by others.

"The full force of our de- ductive processes and the weight of our entire culture will be brought to bear on solving this atrocity."

"Outrage ... atrocity ... best get yourself a thesaurus, Dina, old son," Wolfe murmured, then returned to the com.

"We call on all Federation officials and worlds to assist us in discovering the villains responsible for ..."

*

"What in the name of several hells are you trying to pull off?" Cisco said. "Are you and your goddamned Al'ar buddy on some kind of vendetta?"

"Now, Cisco," Wolfe said mildly, "use some of that Chitet logic that FI's so permeated with these days, and don't get your bowels in an uproar."

"All right." Cisco took a deep breath. "What were—are you trying to accomplish trying to kill the head of the Chitet? I assume you know you missed him."

"I wasn't trying to kill him," Wolfe said. "If I was, he'd be in his meat crate. Think, man."

Cisco shook his head. "I don't get it. Or you."

"I'll just give you one thing you might get out of what happened. Look around. See who's frothing at the mouth in your organization. That might help you pick out a couple more moles. Looks like you've got more of them than a fruitcake's got fruit."

Cisco smiled tightly. "Thanks for helping me clean up my organization. I'm sure you're doing it strictly out of altruism."

"That's me," Wolfe agreed. "Aren't you glad you looked me up last year when I was in a quiet sort of retirement?" His forced smile vanished. "Goddammit, Cisco, you built this monster. You're going to have to live with him, until it's over."

"And when is that? What are you looking for? What are you after?"

Wolfe brought himself under control. "I'll tell you . . . when I figure it out. Right now, I'm still on the trail. The only reason I bothered to contact you was to tell you to keep your gunsels off my ass. I'm on to something, and it's very big."

"With the Al'ar. How does he figure into it?"

"I won't answer that, either way. Maybe because I don't know."

"So what am I supposed to do? Just sit here, listening to all the frigging whines from Earth Central, and nothing more?" Cisco demanded.

"No. I want you to keep watching the Chitet. If you hear of them getting close to me, let me know. You can use this same conduit. I'm monitoring it, through cutouts, about every E-week. But don't try to put a tracer on it.

"Cisco, you sent me down this rathole like a good little terrier, so you can goddamned well sit there with your net and see what comes out."

"And not do anything, no matter what you decide to do? What comes next, Wolfe? Are you going to nuke Federation Control?"

The tight smile came back to Wolfe's face. "Extreme times call for extreme measures, Cisco. I heard you say that, three or four times."

"That was during the war!"

"Like you told me a year ago: Maybe mine's gone on longer than yours."

Wolfe blanked the com without signing off. "He's really going to hammer his arteries when those guys come out of the jungle with the rest of the story."

*

"We are now," Taen said, **"three jumps from entering what were Al'ar sectors. An interesting note, one that I think should be disquieting to us both: I experienced that strange buzzing sound once more when I was waiting for your signal to send the ship down against the Chitets. But it *felt* very faint, very distant.**

"This last sleep period I felt it once more. It was much stronger. This suggests that whatever is causing this is either in the Al'ar sectors or is just beyond them."

"I wonder why I didn't feel it when you did," Wolfe said. "And I wonder if we're the only two people in the galaxy who have.

"You're right. I don't like your information at all."

*

Noted Magician, Mystic, Killed in Mysterious Fire

Press for More

BALTIMORE, EARTH— Leslie Richardson, 63, better known as "The Great Deceiver," was found dead in his houseboat moored not far from this city on the Patapsco River. He died, police said, of mysterious burns, possibly incurred by a freak lightning strike on his boat, although the craft showed no signs of fire damage.

Richardson acquired great fame as an illusionist before and during the war, and was honored for having devoted the War Years to touring and entertaining Federation troops.

He said he owed this to the Federation because he had been working on Glayfer XIX when the Al'ar landed and was briefly a captive of the aliens. He was freed when a surprise counterattack drove the Al'ar from the planet.

After the war, he announced, through his then-manager, that "the illusions I've worked for all these years have lifted the veil," and he retired from performing to devote his life to contemplation and writing about "Other Worlds" he said he could catch dim glimpses of through fasting and meditation.

The Great Deceiver was known for his charm and self-deprecating humor as well as for his famed tricks, one of which, the ability to seemingly become invisible in the midst of a crowd, has never been duplicated by anyone.

He is survived by . . .

*

"Exiting N-space. One jump short of reaching point projected from battles."

"Thanks," Wolfe said.

Taen lifted grasping organs, set them back on his rack. **"I find it what you would term** amusing **that you express gratitude to your machine. It seems a thorough waste of energy."**

"You're right. And I'm polite to you, as well. Ship, do you detect any sign of life?"

"Negative."

"Do you detect any planets, asteroids, any habitable place?"

"Negative."

"Are there any signs of broadcast on any frequency?"

"Negative."

"Make the final jump when you're able."

"Understood."

*

The world was cold, bleak, forbidding.

Wolfe looked again at the screen, then away from the

gray and black wasteland. "What's the environment like?"

"Slight traces of oxygen. Not enough to support human life. Gravity half E-normal. Do you wish geological, atmospheric data?"

"No." He looked at other screens showing the far-distant sun and the other two planets in the system, both frost giants.

"Do you detect any transmissions, any broadcast sign of life?"

"Negative."

"This makes no sense. There's a planet here, as close to Point Zed as possible, and it's deader than God."

"I suggest we make a circumnavigation," Taen said. **"The Guardians, if they are, or were ever, here, would hardly blazon their presence to the heavens."**

"Ship . . . do as he says."

"Understood."

*

"I am afraid you were correct. This world has never seen habitation," Taen said.

"Maybe . . ." Wolfe closed his eyes and let the Lumina carry him to the screen, through it to the desolation below. "Ship," he said. "Turn through 180 degrees, then descend two hundred feet."

"Understood."

"What are you attempting?"

"Pure bluff. As if we just saw something."

"I have a launch," the ship announced unnecessarily as a rock outcropping spat fire at them. *"I am taking standard evasive—"*

"Cancel," Wolfe snapped. "Turn hard into the direction of the missile! Drop one hundred feet."

"Understood," the ship said, and the gravity twisted, contorted, *"but this is contrary to my programming."*

"Full power now!"

"Understood."

The missile, a gray-black tube with an adder's flattened head, flashed at them, past, and Wolfe thought he could see the alien lettering along its sides.

"Not prox-detonated," he said, "or—"

Steering jets flashed along the missile's flanks, and it rolled, then spun wildly, an aelopile, smashing into the ground just below the skimming *Grayle.*

"There's somebody home," Wolfe said, hanging on to the control panel. "Is there any way we can send flowers and gentle words?"

"I do not know of any."

"Ship, get us the hell over the horizon. Full secondary."

"Understood."

"As soon as we're—"

"I have a second launch."

"Damnation! Stand by to launch missile."

"Weapons station ready."

Wolfe hurried across the control deck and swung down a control station.

"Launch the missile," he ordered. "I have it under manual control."

"Understood."

"Shadow Warrior, this is foolish," Taen said. **"You cannot think as fast as a ship-slayer."**

"I'm not planning on thinking," Joshua said. "Now shut up."

He *felt* the Lumina, forced away his own fear, tension.
Breathe . . . you are the void . . . you are the fire . . .

He was out, beyond the ship, riding just ahead of the blast wave of his missile, barely aware of his hands moving on the control panel as the missile came up and around toward the oncoming Al'ar rocket.

Touch the void, be part, be all, reach out, feel . . .

His awareness flashed out once more, floated above the crags as the long double-finned Al'ar ship-killer flashed toward him, then *felt* his own missile beside him.

Hands coming together, fingers outstretched . . .

Far away, in a safe, warm world, Wolfe's hands left the missile's control panel, splayed, moved together, and he heard Taen's hiss of alarm.

Touching . . .

Wolfe's missile veered into the path of the oncoming projectile, and flame balled over nothingness, then vanished, and a few, tiny metal fragments spun down toward the rocks below.

Wolfe stood over the missile controls. Taen was out of his rack, halfway across the compartment.

"Don't bother," Wolfe said. "It's dead. I killed it. Ship, get us the hell off this world. We've got some rethinking to do. I've had enough of this nonsense."

"How was that done?" the Al'ar said. **"I knew you could project your awareness, but how could you affect what your rocket did without touching anything?"**

"I don't know. But I knew, as I took the controls of the rocket, that I could do it."

The Al'ar stared at Wolfe. His hood flared suddenly.

"Shadow Warrior," he said after a time, "now I feel fear toward you. I no longer know what you are, what you are becoming."

* **CHAPTER TEN** *

Taen and Wolfe muscled the cylinder out of the lock, hastily set up its tripod legs, and ran for the nearby rocks as the *Grayle* lifted away into space. The cylinder slid three antennae out, and one swiveled up toward the sky.

The two space-suited beings stumbled on, moving as fast as the bulky suits and their heavy pack frames and slung blast rifles would let them. Wolfe kept glancing at the hillcrest. They'd made about a quarter of a mile when Wolfe saw the flicker of movement, knocked the Al'ar down, and flattened beside him.

A double-finned missile arced over the nearby hilltop and smashed into the cylinder. Smoke, fire flared up, and rock dust obscured the clearing.

Long moments later, it settled. There was a crater about thirty feet deep surrounded by splintered boulders.

Wolfe got to his feet, licking blood from his lip where the blast had smashed his head into the rim of his faceplate. He unclipped a lead from his suit and plugged it into an improvised connection on Taen's armor.

"I guess they told us."

"Your diversion was clever."

"We'll see if it fooled them into thinking we just dropped the sensor and scooted, or not. Then it's clever. But I sure hate to lose that snooper. Damned thing cost me too many credits to just throw away."

"Would you rather have thrown away your life?"

"Nope. But I wish I wasn't such a stickler for authenticity and had thrown them the spare toilet instead." Wolfe checked monitors. "How thoughtful. It wasn't a nuke they dumped on us. Shall we press on and see what else the lion has protecting his den?"

"When you speak to other Terrans, do you also attempt to confuse them?"

"As often as possible." Wolfe turned serious. "Taen, do you have any sense of whether we're going after some robot deathtrap, or is there intelligence, such as maybe your Guardians, inside?"

"I do not know."

"Second question. How many ways are they going to try to kill us? Anything besides the usual Al'ar methods?"

"I do not know that, either."

"Elaborate."

"Toward the close of the war, when we realized the Federation was slowly closing the trap, we experimented with many different types of weapons. I was not taken into the confidence of our leaders, so I do not know what devices may have been successful enough to be taken out of the laboratories and put in production."

"You bring utter peace and confidence to my soul. Come on. We've got some hills to hike."

*

Chitet Murder Charges Rock Federation Master Speaker Athelstan: "Government Tried to Assassinate Me."

<u>Press for More</u>

BATAN—Chitet Master Speaker Matteos Athelstan today accused the Federation of masterminding a plot to murder him in last month's suicide-crash of a starship into his palace.

The ship has now been identified as being the Exploration Vessel *Occam*, an ex-Federation warship disarmed and converted by the Chitet two years ago. It was reported missing on a routine venture two months before it dove into Speaker Athelstan's Residency, and had been assumed lost with all hands.

However, three days ago the surviving crew arrived at a mining camp on the Outlaw World of Triumphant, and claimed that they had been hijacked by a Federation spy-ship of the *Sorge* class.

According to documents sent to this com, the *Occam*'s Master, Captain Millet, said they were following their orders when a Federation vessel identifying itself as the *Harnack* ordered it to cut its drive. Captain Millet of course obeyed. The *Harnack* then connected airlocks to the Chitet ship and, when the lock was open, Federation sailors coldly murdered four of Captain Millet's crewmen and seized the ship.

They were imprisoned in a hold and then released, with minimal supplies, on a dangerous jungle world, no doubt, Master Speaker Athelstan said, in the hopes they would be destroyed by the savage beasts of that planet.

However, due to the inspired leadership of Captain Millet and the other officers, the crew was able to . . .

*

Wolfe slid to the knife-edge of the ridge, peered over, and quickly ducked back.

The fortress sprawled across the hill beyond them, although little could be seen aboveground. But the knolls were a little too regular, the mounds winding between them too convenient.

He reconnected the com lead to Taen's suit. "We're on it. How do we get inside?"

"We fight our way in," the Al'ar said. **"I know of no way of communicating with whoever is inside, nor would they be likely to believe me, especially as I'm in the company of a Terran."**

"In the old holopics," Wolfe grumbled, "I'd pretend to be your prisoner and then we'd jump 'em. Pity you come from a race that doesn't believe in silliness like that."

"Why should anyone bother taking an enemy alive, unless killing captives makes the others fight more fiercely, as Terrans do? Certainly we never concerned ourselves with our own prisoners."

"I know," Wolfe said. "But they vanished along with everybody else. Forget it. Why haven't they opened up on us? Surely they've got IR sensors."

"Perhaps, perhaps not. Perhaps they are waiting to see what our move will be, or perhaps they are waiting for us to move into the open."

Wolfe thought for a moment, then wriggled out of his pack. He took out a small tube, opened it, and took out a small, slim rocket. As the rocket came free, guidance fins snapped out of slots. He carefully pried at the tube and stripped five metal rods from it.

He clipped these into slots on the tube to form a launching rack.

"We've been where we are too long," he said. "Move over to behind that boulder there. And we won't need to be careful about anybody homing on our signals once the shooting starts."

He unhooked the com cable and reeled it back into his suit. He ran awkwardly about thirty yards, set the rack down, slid the rocket into position, came back. Then he took what looked like binocs, except with an extra barrel in the center, from his pack and slithered back up to the ridgecrest.

Wolfe focused the viewer, put the crosshairs on one of the knolls, touched a stud on its side, then a second.

The small rocket shot into the air. Following the homing signal, it shattered against the knoll, a surprisingly large explosion for so small a device.

Instantly the knoll unmasked a multitube weapon, sending laser fire spattering in the direction the rocket had come from.

A moment later, a second pillbox exposed itself and put crossfire into the same area.

Joshua backslid into cover. "Maybe they *don't* have infrared," he said, putting his pack back on and crouching across to where Taen waited.

"Did you mark those two?"

"I did."

"Now it gets interesting. Did you ever take part in an infantry assault?"

"Never. My fighting was in space or in-atmosphere."

"That doesn't improve my mood." Wolfe took off his pack, took out two round grenades, one anodized white, the other red, and an egg-shaped object almost as large as his head. He twisted a dial at the top. "When I charge, you put one burst on that first pillbox, then concentrate on the second."

"That sounds extraordinarily hazardous for you."

Wolfe shrugged. "It's about the only way to take out interlocking fire. But if anybody else starts shooting at me, discourage them. Try not to get killed."

"That is not my desire at the moment."

Wolfe thumbed the first grenade's activator, over-armed it into the open space in front of them, came to his feet, and ran forward. As he came into the open, he pitched the second grenade to his front, underhand, just as the first exploded and smoke boiled.

A moment later the second grenade blasted a flare of energy. Wolfe saw Taen's weapon fire past him, saw return fire from one of the turrets, then hurled the egg-shaped object high into the air.

It hit just short of the first pillbox, exploded, and the turret blew up, metal disguised as rock tearing with a screech audible above the crack of Taen's fire and the blind return blasts from the second pillbox.

He dove forward into smoke, feeling rounds smash into rock a foot away, pulled another grenade from its pouch, touched its stud and threw.

Again fire flashed and Wolfe, lungs searing, stumbled up, unslinging his blast rifle, and ran past the flare, sending rapid-fire bursts toward the second weapons bunker.

An explosion sent him tumbling, arm coming up to protect his faceplate. Another turret must have unmasked—a rocky column above him shattered and cascaded down.

Wolfe rolled twice, came up, and sent a burst at the weapons station, then *felt* death behind him and went flat.

A blade slashed as he rolled and saw a six-legged gray metalloid spider rearing over him.

The scythe on one arm lashed down and smashed his blast rifle as Wolfe yanked his pistol from its holster, fired twice.

The blasts took the spider in its leg segments, and the

robot thrashed, toppled, as the Al'ar pillbox "saw" movement and blew its carapace into fragments.

A moment later, Taen's weapon blasted the third pillbox into silence.

Coming from between the rocks were three more of the robots. Each was about eight feet tall, with a body like a round cigar and a small dome on top with a weapons tube jutting from it.

Wolfe knelt, held his pistol in a two-handed grip, and sent bolts smashing into the first. It shuddered, side-stepped, came on.

The one behind it reared as a ray from Taen's weapon took it head-on, and his second burst seared its belly open, revealing multicolored circuitry.

Wolfe sent a grenade spinning at the first, and the blast went off under it, seemingly harmlessly. But the robot froze in midstride, then sagged to the rocks.

The last spider was on Wolfe, cutting at him. Wolfe ducked, had its metalloid arm in his hands, trying to twist it. Inexorable force twisted, sent him down, and the scythe inched toward his faceplate.

Breathe . . . fire, burning all, blazing, wildfire, firestorm, beyond control . . .

He felt muscles tear, and the robot's arm bent, metal scraping. Wolfe rolled forward, came to his hands and knees under the nightmare, then stood, lifting against the greasy underside of the spider, pushing up, and the robot flipped onto its back, legs flailing.

Joshua saw his pistol, had it, and sent the rest of the magazine smashing into the robot as its legs flexed and died.

Taen was beside him. **"It is gone. And you are hurt."**

Suddenly Wolfe was aware of pain in his side, looked

down, saw the black where a blast had burned his suit, and felt his suit's air hissing out.

He fumbled at his waist, but Taen's grasping organs were ahead of him, opening the patch and sealing the suit.

Wolfe swayed, and the Al'ar pulled him into the shelter of some boulders as another turret opened fire. The fire spattered harmlessly against boulders.

Breathe . . . breathe . . .

"Are you injured?"

Wolfe *felt* his body, shook his head, then realized Taen could not see the gesture.

"No. Not badly. Burned a little. Sorry. But I just lost my fondness for goddamned spiders."

"Those devices surprised me," Taen said. **"I had heard no stories of their development. I would guess they were completely experimental, since it was so easy to deactivate them."**

"Easy for you to say," Wolfe said. "All right. We're inside their first line of defense. Let me see what I can discover."

He sat, awkwardly.

Breathe . . . welcome the void . . . there is no pain . . . there is no fear . . . earth and water combine, restore your body . . . now reach beyond, find hei, *let* hei *surround you.*

Without realizing it his gauntleted hands touched, tried to link fingers.

He was above the planet's stony surface, looking down, looking at, looking through.

Here are weapons stations . . . here passageways . . . here there are . . .

Wolfe came back to his body's awareness, felt the flush of strength, energy, peace wash over him.

"Now we shall enter their fortress." For some reason, it was natural to speak in Al'ar.

He took another, longer tube from his pack and got to his feet. Taen began to say something, fell silent.

They went between boulders, Wolfe dimly aware of something shooting, no awareness of where the blasts were striking. He went flat and crawled for almost fifty yards behind the cover of one of the mounded passageways.

Joshua came to an open space, hesitated, held up one hand for Taen to wait, went across the open space very fast.

Nothing happened. Wolfe beckoned, and Taen stumbled after him. He'd barely gained the shelter of a low cluster of rocks when a laser-blast shattered splinters behind him.

Taen looked at Wolfe and saw eyes staring, fixed on some strange invisible eternity through the faceplate.

Joshua's fingers moved automatically on the tube, and one end extruded until it was nearly four feet long. He opened a tiny compartment on the side of the tube, took what looked like a jeweler's eyepiece connected to an electrical lead, and positioned it in the center of his suit's faceplate.

He moved Taen out of the way, then stood, tube on one shoulder. It swept back and forth, then held steady on an open, completely unremarkable rocky patch.

Wolfe touched the firing stud and the rocket blasted out, flame spouting from the rear of the launch tube. The rocket exploded, smoke and flame gouting. Through the boil, they saw where the hidden hatch had been ripped open.

Wolfe tossed the launcher tube aside.

"**Come,**" he ordered, and Taen followed.

The hatch was only open about a foot, exposing a ramp, blackness. There wasn't room to squeeze through.

Wolfe took the hatch, hunched, and lifted. Metal shrieked, but the ramp did not move.

Taen was beside him, grasping organs beside human fingers. Wolfe felt resistance give, and the hatch shrieked open another foot.

Wolfe half pushed Taen through, followed him down.

Joshua *saw* clearly, led the way down twenty feet to where the ramp ended at a T-intersection, pulled Taen into it just as an automatic hatch slid across the rampway.

The silence came like a curtain of rain across Wolfe's mind.

He unsealed his faceplate, sucked clean, sterile air, *knowing* the fortress' atmosphere was still present.

"**Welcome home, Taen,**" he said.

Taen opened his suit, as well.

"**No,**" he said. "**I am not home. But I have reached a waystation on the journey.**"

His voice echoed down the cold metal corridor.

They started down its curving length, moving carefully, weapons ready. They'd gone about seventy yards when, without warning, the deck fell away below them.

* CHAPTER ELEVEN *

Joshua rolled until he was falling facedown, then used his suit's steering jets to stabilize out of the beginnings of a spin. Craning his neck to the side, he saw Taen floating about three feet above him.

The Al'ar drew level with him and Wolfe realized their rate of descent was slowing. They'd dropped about five hundred feet and were falling at no more than a few feet per second when Joshua saw a deck looming below. He kick-snapped erect and bent his legs for the landing.

No impact came as the fortress' antigrav caught, held them. As they touched down, a metal roof crashed across, sealing off the tunnel they'd fallen down.

"Alice, and friend. Canned for the feast," Joshua said. Taen did not respond, but scanned the walls and decks of the oval-shaped trap. Both still had weapons ready.

"I see nothing that suggests weakness that might be cut away," Taen said.

"Nor I," Joshua agreed. He tried to *feel* out, beyond. Through three-quarters of the arc, he could *feel* nothing but metal, rock. On the fourth, his *vision* went beyond, but only into emptiness. Then it met something and was hurled back.

Joshua shuddered, as if he'd been struck.

"What was that?" Taen asked.

"Somebody out there doesn't want to be watched," Wolfe said.

"Lay down the weapons," came a voice. It filled his mind and the tiny room.

Wolfe hesitated, noticed Taen had knelt, set his weapon down, did the same.

He *felt* someone, several beings, *watching* him, and squirmed, not comfortable.

The section of the wall slid open, and five Al'ar were in the opening. Two held long, slender weapons identical to Taen's. The other three wore dark ceremonial robes. The one in the center wore a Lumina stone on a metallic headband. He *knew* all of them to be Guardians.

"Name yourself."

"Taen."

"The One Who Fights From Shadows is the name I was given many years ago by another Guardian," Wolfe said. **"In Terran,** Joshua Wolfe."

He felt his own Lumina warm as the Al'ar *reached* toward him.

Then the stone became cold as the Guardian turned to Taen. **"My senses did not tell me that another of us had remained behind."**

Taen made no reply.

"Why did you not make The Crossing with the others?"

"I do not know. Perhaps I was unworthy."

The Guardian began to speak, stopped, as if rethinking his words, then went on: **"You have spent time among these others, these groundlings. You have let your** mind become corrupt. There was no 'worth' to those who have gone, no 'shame' to those who have remained here."

"And how was I to sense this?"

Wolfe blinked, thinking for an instant he'd detected impossible pain in Taen's words.

"If you did not go, then we must assume there is intent to your remaining. Perhaps it has to do with this one who accompanies you.

"Neither of you is the other's prisoner. You are working as a pair, as a conjoined unit? I find this a concept beyond visualization."

"Nevertheless," Taen said, "it exists."

The Guardian's attention shifted to Wolfe. "I am puzzled by the responses of this young one. Perhaps you might assist me in clarifying the murky pool."

"I doubt that," Wolfe said. "I myself have little clarity of thought."

"What do you seek?"

Joshua said nothing but slowly shook his head.

"Perhaps I can answer for both of us," Taen said. "I began this search, looking for the Guardians, even though there was little but rumors. I sought to find why I was abandoned, and to be allowed either death or to join the others.

"This one, whom I had known when we were hatchlings, and whom I fought against in the time of war, joined me. What he hopes to gain, what he hoped to gain by studying our way in the time before war, I cannot tell you. But he was a strong pupil, both in the ways of fighting and in the ways of thinking. Since we have been together, he has become an adept, having talents even I was not aware could be gained. But I leap ahead.

"Before we could truly begin our search, we *felt* a threat, something unseen, unknown. Its onset is a buzzing, as of insects, but there is not true sound. I have felt an aura of blue when this happens; he has not. He has had some pain, some physical evidence, his outer layer showing bruises for a time accompanied by sharp pain, then the signs vanish.

"Both of us *felt* this had something to do with our quest, and feel this menace growing, and feel it especially strongly here in these parts of space that were once Al'ar."

As Taen spoke, Wolfe felt an emanation from the first Guardian, then the others—something dark, strange, cold. Taen flinched as if he'd been struck, and Joshua realized he, too, had felt what the Guardians had emitted.

"So," Taen said, "we were not becoming insane. This is real. What is it?"

The Guardian looked at his two fellows, then back at Taen and Wolfe. "This shall be explained. But not at this moment. You. Terran. I cannot bid you welcome as an honored one. Our races fought too long and there was too much blood spilt for me to feel or say that. But you are now our guest. You will eat, sleep, learn here, and no one shall bring you harm or offer you shame. I am Jadera."

The Guardian bowed slightly, and the Lumina on his headband flared, subsided.

Wolfe's vision blurred inexplicably, cleared when he blinked moisture from them.

He realized there was a smile on his face.

*

Wolfe half remembered some of the foods they ate, but most were unfamiliar. They were the dishes of a state dinner, which no youth, even the son of an ambassador, would have been allowed. Some he liked, a few he had to force down, fingers crossed as his mind reminded him there was nothing in the Al'ar diet a Terran could not survive.

He wondered what the Al'ar foods tasted like to the aliens. To him, they were a flurry of flavors, mingling or sometimes overriding each other. Some were solid, but most were in heavy soups. A few came in covered, insulated containers, and were inhaled as a gas.

The room he ate in was huge, shadowed. Against the walls light-constructs flared, subsided. Beside each seat was a half dome on the table that delivered and removed each dish.

The Al'ar ate at small tables around him, conversing in low tones. Joshua wryly reminded himself the unemotional Al'ar were genetically incapable of performing a Prodigal Son routine and that he was the only one who was upset that Taen's arrival wasn't made more of.

At first he thought all of the aliens on the planet had been summoned, but then he realized many of them were present only in image.

He quietly asked Taen how this was done.

"A simple matter," Taen said. **"Each sits in a booth with a background prepared to simulate this room. There is a communications device in front of him, and he has large screens around him. This way, we do not shrivel in loneliness, even though we are great distances apart at our duties."**

Wolfe turned to Jadera. **"If it is a permitted question, what are the duties of the Guardians on this planet?"**

"You may ask, and I shall answer. There are many, ranging from maintaining this fortress to keeping watch for intruders to ... the matter that brought you here, and that which I shall speak of at another time. Still others have rituals to attend to."

"Rituals?" Wolfe asked. **"But we Terrans always believed—I do not know why—the Guardians were leaders of the flesh, not what we would term** priests."

Taen lifted a grasping organ, expressing surprise at what Joshua said.

"But how could that be?" Jadera responded before Taen could speak. **"How can a being lead in the body if he has not a vision, an ability to lead in the spirit?"**

"Quite well," Joshua said. **"Every time we Terrans have had someone like that, we end up killing each other over which god is the better."**

"I have heard of this," Jadera said. **"But it makes no sense. I have had it explained as what you Terrans call a god but understand it only as a concept in the mind, not reality. How could there be an argument, when there is but one truth?"**

"How could there *not* be an argument," Wolfe countered, **"when every believer in truth I have known or read of seems to think that truth belongs exclusively to him and his friends?"**

"I guess we were foredoomed to war against each other," Jadera said.

Wolfe's attention was drawn to a table not far from his, a strangely carved, octagonal piece of furniture. At it sat an Al'ar of great age. His corpselike pallor was mottled, marred.

When he saw Wolfe looking at him, his hood flared to its full size, his grasping organ touched a stud, and the Al'ar and where he sat vanished.

Jadera had noted what occurred. **"That was Cerigo. He is one who holds firmly to the old ways, and believes that we should have fought you the instant our races came in contact rather than waiting. He also lost his entire brood-cluster in the war, so he has little ability to stand the sight of Terrans."**

"And I lost those who bred me as well," Wolfe said softly. "Yet I still am sitting here. Perhaps his . . . truth is lacking in some areas."

Jadera said nothing.

"Then we are what you call shamed," Taen said in Terran, then returned to Al'ar. **"Please do not dwell on Cerigo and his behavior unless you must."**

Wolfe shrugged and turned back to his plate.

After a time, Jadera spoke again. **"When you were given your Al'ar name, did the Guardian who gave you that name tell you its history, or of the one he must have been thinking of when he bestowed it on you?"**

"No," Wolfe said, startled. **"I did not know of any such."**

"That is odd," Jadera said. **"If he had not gone before, if he had not made the Crossing, I would inquire why not. When one of us is given his adult name, it is only after a long consultation, and the hatchling is given the opportunity to study the past and either accept or reject the name as being fitting."**

"Perhaps," Taen said, "it was because he was unsure of whether it was right to bestow a name on this one even though he was an honest Seeker of the Way. That Guardian, whose name I must not use, since he is gone, hesitated, and I was forced to remind him that the codex had been consulted and such a thing was not forbidden, even though it had not been done within memory. Perhaps he intended to give the history to this One Who Fights From Shadows at a later time. Perhaps the war prevented that from occurring."

"But still," Jadera said. "The naming ceremony was not proper."

He sat motionless for a moment. "This must be rectified before any other matters can be dealt with, since one presses closely on the other."

*

When the meal was finished, the Al'ar sat silently for a time, as was their custom.

Wolfe had done the same as a boy, among the Al'ar who taught him, and the old feeling of warmth, of belonging, came as he sat, still in voice and mind, among the Guardians.

Then, one by one, the projected visions of those elsewhere on the planet blinked out.

Jadera rose. "I shall show you a burrow that we have modified as suitable for you."

Another Al'ar led Taen away, and Joshua followed Jadera.

The chamber was octagonal, with a ceiling in various shades of purple that curved slightly downward at the corners. Where the resting rack would have been, soft, circular pillows in various colors had been piled inside a framework.

There was a table against one wall; a cup and a flask of some liquid sat on it.

"Is this satisfactory?" Jadera inquired. **"Does this not shame us? We have done the best we know, but we never envisioned a Terran as anything other than . . . as being our guest."**

Joshua noted with amusement that a covered vessel and a neat pile of soft clothes was set discreetly in one corner. **"More than sufficient."**

Jadera held out his grasping organs, turned, and left. Joshua yawned, undressed, and lay down on the pillows, wondering what they were normally used for.

His hand stretched out and found the empty holster his gun should have been in. A thought came that this was one of the few times in many years a weapon hadn't been ready at hand, yet he felt no anxiety.

Then he closed his eyes and sleep dropped like a curtain about his mind.

*

Wolfe was asleep, but not asleep. He dreamed, but what came and went in his mind were not dreams.

*

The universe his sac opened in was not the one he had known. It was already old, decaying toward rebirth.

*

He had a memory of those who'd chosen to breed him, and of those other adults who cared for his cluster as they swarmed, grew, fed, played.

Wolfe, dreaming, tried to feel happiness, contentment, anger, laughter, could not.

There was but satisfaction at being fed, at besting another or of helping another of the cluster against a third, then the lesser satisfaction of helping another better "him"self.

He was Al'ar.

*

There were places set aside for hatchlings where no adult went. Some were mountainous, some covered with many breeds of ferns, from tiny ones that crumpled in his grasping organs to ones that towered above him and hid the sky. Other places had lakes and islands.

The hatchlings went into these places and formed groups or lived singly, doing as they had seen adults do, attempting those tasks adults did and they would do in their turn.

They fought, one against one, one against several, several against one.

Hatchlings died, but this was as it should be so the race would grow, would increase, would progress.

The one who had not yet been given a name killed more than most, and this was noted, both by his elders and other clusters.

*

There were five of them. When the third moon set, they met outside the cave their cluster was living in. They knew the direction to take, had walked most of it during daylight, thinking of other things so as not to alarm the hatchling who carried death with him.

That one without a name had built a burrow that was not a burrow but a challenge, foolishly, on the banks of a flowing waterway, with little cover and few places to flee other than into the water. But even the current would carry him toward the dens of beasts that would feed on Al'ar.

He had built a low fire from minerals he'd dug from the bank, under what the Wolfe-dreamer thought was a leafless tree carved of stone but was something that lived and grew.

The five stopped at the last bit of groundcover and looked long at the guttering fire and the motionless shadow of the one who seemed to have no fear.

They communicated in touches, grasping organs signaling who was to go forward, who was to come from the side, who was to wait until he was immobilized and then deal the killing stroke.

The one who had been chosen leader lifted his grasping organ, hood flaring, about to give the signal.

He came at them from behind, where he'd stalked them from when they left their cave.

The first died as a grasping organ darted into an eye socket, and "blood" oozed, the second as a knee took "her" in the back of the head, snapping the grouped tendons that was an Al'ar spine. The third swung with a club, missed as his target vanished, reappeared out of reach, and the club smashed into the fourth's chest. The last, the leader, had time to snap out a kick that sent the attacker stumbling.

The two from the cave came at him from either side.

The one Wolfe dreamed he was jumped straight up, turned and both his legs snapped out. He felt the kick land, felt body organs crush, felt death come.

The last turned to flee, but somehow the attacker was in front of him, slits of his eyes burning, fire demanding fuel, and the last one's spirit was that fuel and there were five young Al'ar sprawled dead, not far from a dying fire and a waterway.

*

It was not long after that the Choices were made. Some chose to breed, some chose to accept breeding. The tasks of the future were clear, and each picked the one he'd been called to as his lifework.

He had known forever what his own task would be.

Warrior.

Guardians further tested him, taught him.

Then they gave him a Lumina to hold, and a new name, honoring what he had done in the night, in the desolation.

He was the One Who Fights From Shadows.

There was no greater honor for an Al'ar than to be a warrior, except to be chosen as a Guardian.

*

He learned other skills while he refined those of the body. He learned the use of weapons, those that the Wolfe-dreamer could name as knife, gun, missile, others that had no name or image to him.

More important, he learned when not to fight but to flee or to dissemble and lie until the weight lay on his side.

He learned how to use vehicles that let him fly, both in various kinds of atmosphere as well as space.

He was taught how to help a ship transition from one part of the great Al'ar Empire to another.

Finally he was ready.

He was named a Keeper of Order, on the far edges of the Al'ar space. Here he would be in charge of the lives of the lesser beings the Al'ar ruled, beings of many planets and thoughts, but none of real worth.

Wolfe stirred, half woke, muttered in protest, then returned to the "dream."

The One Who Fights From Shadows knew the codex and ruled firmly, giving all as much life as he thought necessary, and bringing it to an end when the time for that came, as well.

Time passed.

Then the changes began.

Worlds fell out of contact with the parent culture.

Sometimes a handful of ships managed to flee to momentary safety, but as often as not the Al'ar inside them were dead or had twisted minds that could no longer make sense.

Other Al'ar Keepers of Order went into darkness, with no explanation for their death.

Something had come into their galaxy, something strange, something deadly, something unutterably alien.

Wolfe, in his dream, tried to feel *what that threat was, tried to* see *it, but his thrust was turned aside.*

The One Who Fights From Shadows was summoned to a great conference. All of the Al'ar homeworlds were linked together.

They were told the worst.

The Al'ar were doomed.

That which had entered their galaxy would be their destruction.

They could either stand and fight, or flee.

The Guardians had found a way to transition through space-time into another place, a place where they could not, would not be followed.

There was no debate, no reason for discussion. The path was clear.

To gain time, it would be necessary for some Al'ar, the best warriors, the strongest Keepers of Order, to counterattack, to hold back the evil until their people could escape.

The One Who Fought From Shadows knew he was one of the lucky ones and was lifted higher than others with the knowledge.

He was trained again, this time by Guardians, in ways to make his mind, his will harder than any metalloid, sharper than any blade or ray.

Special ships were built for the Keepers who would go out to that final battle, ships that dwarfed the biggest Al'ar battleships, but each crewed by only one being.

These ships had a single purpose, a single enemy.

The One Who Fights From Shadows was in the first group. He leapt from change-point to change-point among the stars, each time knowing he was closer to the unseen enemy.

He came into "real" space from his last vaulting point, and the enemy hung in space before him, a dark cloud blocking the stars it had already killed.

His grasping organs swept over weapons banks, and wave after wave of long-strikers shot forth.

He *felt* them strike home, *felt* the enemy's agony.

Far behind him, half across the galaxy, he knew the first of his people were preparing to flee to safety.

Then his foe regained strength and reached out, through space, through metal, for him, and took him, held him.

The One Who Fights From Shadows knew a moment, an eternity of red torment, fire, cried out, was no more.

*

Joshua Wolfe woke, shouting in pain, a dull buzzing in his mind. His arms, legs, and stomach were seared with red welts.

* CHAPTER TWELVE *

"How was that done?" Wolfe demanded.

"Fairly simply," Jadera said. "There are records of events. We know you possess a Lumina and have become skilled in its use. We used one of our own as a link and gave you the life of the honored one who previously bore your name."

Joshua grimaced, caught a reflection of himself in a polished wall panel, looked away. His eyes were deeply shadowed, his newly young countenance pallid from the night's "dream."

"So you—the Al'ar—were driven from your own universe into this one?"

"Exactly."

"And now this . . . thing, whatever it is, is in our own space-time?"

"Not yet. But it threatens."

"What is it? I could not determine."

"We did not permit you to see. Now we shall. Follow me."

"May I accompany you?" Taen asked.

"No," Jadera said.

"Why is this not possible?" Wolfe asked. "Is there

danger? Taen is my partner. It would be good for him to have all knowledge that I do."

"There could be some danger," Jadera replied. "But it is not that. We try to avoid contact with ... with what you are going to encounter. There is an Al'ar saying: 'The scent of the falaas attracts the food-gatherer.' "

"Or," Joshua said, "in Terran, 'The bleating of the kid excites the tiger.' "

"Just so."

It took a moment for Wolfe to realize that Jadera had understood him. He started to comment, changed his mind, and followed the Guardian out the chamber door and to a slideway.

*

The room was an irregular polygon. The floor rose and fell in a series of small concave waves, and was flat only in the center. The ceiling was dimpled. The walls were crystalline with colors that were motionless when looked at directly, but shifted prismatically for peripheral vision.

"We shall need your Lumina for this."

Wolfe turned his back, took the egg-shaped gem from its hiding place, a pouch between his legs slung on a thin band around his waist.

Jadera held out his hand, and reluctantly Joshua gave the Lumina to him.

Jadera walked across the humped floor easily, as if it were flat. Wolfe followed, moving carefully.

Jadera set the Lumina down in the center of the flat area, then took two other gems, each a bit larger than Wolfe's, from the pockets of his robes.

"Position yourself on the floor," he ordered. "You

know how to liberate yourself from your body, do you not?"

"I do. But only for a moment."

"Time is of no import now. It has ceased to exist. Once you have freed yourself physically, you will know how to do the rest."

Wolfe sank to his knees, placing both hands, fingers pointed inward, on his thighs. Jadera set the other two Lumina to form a line with Wolfe and his own gem.

"Now the machine is ready.

"Be advised, One Who Fights From Shadows, that what you are going to see is not real, although I use the word only as a label."

"What is it then?"

Jadera considered his words. "This enemy was not native to our original galaxy, or so it is believed, but comes from yet another time and space. It has more than a fourth-dimensional presence, unlike you and I.

"Therefore, what you will see, all your experiences, will be what your mind and your Terran culture suggests.

"To understand this more completely, imagine that you are a being in only two dimensions, such as in one of your hanging pictures. Now imagine that somehow you are lifted from that picture and inserted into what we call the 'real world.' Forgive my use of this obvious fiction.

"You would be only able to perceive cross-sections of this other, three-dimensional world, so an object, your Lumina, perhaps, would appear as a series of varying-sized ovals, smaller at first, then larger, then smaller as it moved past your perception.

"Similarly, you, who consider yourself a three-dimensional being, perceive the Al'ar in a manner that we are not."

Joshua blinked, began to ask something.

"No. Concentrate on the matter at hand," Jadera said. "Experience all, but remember it is all ultimately false and will give you no more than a hint of what is out there."

He returned to the door and touched the wall in several places. "You may begin to *see* whenever you wish."

He left the room, and the door slid closed behind him.

Breathe . . . breathe . . .

Joshua lifted his hands, fingers splayed, thumb and forefinger touching, in front of his face.

Zai . . . Accept all . . . welcome the universe . . .

Reflexively his fingers came together into knife-edge, interlocked.

The void reaches out . . . accept ku *. . . all is one . . .*

*

He appeared to be in a huge cavern, the walls dank, dripping. It was illuminated by unknown phosphorescence.

The stone under his feet was worn to a wide, smooth path by the passage of numberless beings.

He heard that insect-buzzing once more. It came from ahead of him.

He went down the path, and the buzzing grew louder.

There was a wall visible through the dimness and, in its center, an enormous door.

It was like no door he'd ever seen. It was a dark stone, broken with obsidianlike streaks. It and its frame were carved with symbols and letters Wolfe thought might be an archaic form of Al'ar script. It seemed to open on either side, and above and below.

The buzzing grew louder.

Wolfe reached out, touched the door, felt heat.

The stone shimmered, became opaque, and he was in emptiness. There was a distant galaxy, its stars swirling as if he were seeing it over millions of years.

He was somehow closer, so stars were all around him. There was a scattering of red giants, more white dwarfs, still more dark, burned-out black dwarf stars. In the far distance, he saw the white heat from a pair of supernova.

As he watched, the light flashed, died. Where the supernova had been were neutron stars, falling into collapsars.

This universe was contracting, blue-shifting, dying toward its phoenix rebirth.

The being called Wolfe now saw something strange.

The space between the stars was not dark, was not night, but was filled with millions of minuscule red dots. He could see them pulsing, but they had no light of their own.

He shuddered, feeling fear, feeling death in their swirling life.

He willed himself to move closer, to study them.

Pain washed over him, flaring as if he'd been cast into a great, invisible fire.

Before he could scream, before he could move, he was on the far side of the portal, crouched in a fighting stance in the strangely floored room.

The three Luminas blazed in front of him, not with the usual multicolored lights, but solid red, the same red as he'd seen in that distant galaxy.

Then their light died, and they were nothing more than unimpressive, gray oval stones.

Breathe . . . breathe . . .

Jadera came into the room.

"You have seen." It was not a question.

Wolfe rose, bowed to the three stones. It seemed correct. "I did. That is the universe from which you came?"

"Yes. I assume you also saw some sort of a door, a gateway?"

"I did."

"That represents the rift in space, in time, that we created to leave that universe for this. Because it cannot be sealed we Guardians were created, to stand watch against our ancient enemy. You saw it?"

"I saw something between the stars, in space, that appeared red to me. It had filled the distance between the nearest ones completely but was patchier farther out, toward the ends of the galaxy."

"That was it."

"What is it?"

"Once more, I must remind you, there are no correct words for it. Not in my language, not in yours."

"It reminds me, for some unknown reason," Wolfe said slowly, "of what we call a virus."

"I know the term. Except this virus can take anything, take all for a host, from small, living beings to planets to the space between them. Perhaps it even infects the very fabric of space. Once these things have been touched by our enemy, they become different. If they lived once, they live no longer, at least not in the form we call life. Inanimate objects become part of the creature, the being, as if their particles have been altered to match its own.

"Call it a virus, if that pleases you. It is a single entity; it is many. It bears a resemblance to your microorganism in two other ways—it is all-consuming and it is always growing, increasing."

"I saw but one galaxy. What of the others in that universe?"

"I assume they are 'infected' by this time, since within the last time periods we have been aware that the enemy is looking about for new territory to grow into."

"This universe?"

"Yes."

"So it followed you."

"It has not yet followed us. But it appears aware of our flight, as if we somehow left a trail."

"Thanks," Wolfe said, changing language. "So humanity's next. And we can't run like you Al'ar did."

"What would your people have done if they had our powers and were threatened by this being? Would Terrans have done differently?"

"No," Wolfe admitted. "But what you said doesn't make me feel any fonder of you at the moment."

Jadera remained silent, and Wolfe thought he sensed indifference.

"Can this enemy be fought?" Joshua asked.

"It could have been once."

"You speak in the past. Please explain."

"I shall show you. Come."

*

Taen was waiting in the hall outside. Wolfe quickly explained what had happened.

"**I was told what you would see by another Guardian,**" the Al'ar said. "**I will say I have no regrets at not looking at the enemy who destroyed my people's home and sent us into exile in this terrible universe you inhabit.**"

Wolfe eyed him, made no comment.

Jadera led them into a circular room. A featureless gray column five feet high and a foot in diameter rose to one side. Jadera walked behind it and touched places on the column.

There was darkness and then a huge Lumina appeared. It was about the size of Wolfe's head.

"**This is an image of the Overlord Stone,**" Jadera said, "**the greatest of all Lumina. It is said that all the other stones hived from this one, although how that could be possible is not known.**

"**This stone, like its smaller sisters, is actually little more than a lens, and gives the properly trained adept something on which to focus his powers—even his wishes, if he is of a high enough level—and causes certain events to occur that seem impossible.**

"**The Lumina were native to our original universe. They were used by many generations of Al'ar as tools to help build our powers to fight, to move in hostile environments and times. They are weapons, learning tools, many things, depending on who looks into them, with what desires.**

"**When the enemy appeared, our forefathers were just beginning to use this great Lumina to explore other possible universes. We thought it might even be** possible to enter those of the past and future, although no one had yet accomplished that.

"Then, as I said, the enemy came, and all of our efforts were concentrated on defeating that horror.

"As you dreamed in our records, one was the original One Who Fights From Shadows. He and his fellows died an honorable death giving us valuable time to flee.

"Once we had reached this universe, we tried to close the rift, but were unsuccessful.

"We positioned one of our starships close to the rift and created Guardians to watch for any signs that our enemy might sense us and follow. While a handful of us kept watch, the rest of the Al'ar expanded into this new galaxy and began settling new worlds.

"After some time, we encountered humans.

"We studied your techniques for moving planetoids, improved them, and, about one hundred years ago, positioned this world you are on to replace the Guardians' ship and armed it to be nearly impregnable, although you proved that there is no fortress that cannot be assaulted with success.

"The rest is as you know it.

"Eventually we realized that only one race could exist in this universe, and the other would be doomed to extinction."

"And so you started the war," Wolfe said. "I'll accept you believed you had to wipe us out. But what made you think we were as eager to shed blood as you?"

"That was first prophesied by some of our more conservative elders, beings like Cerigo. We studied

the matter further, and realized that those who pre-
dicted the worst were right, after we found what you
beings did to your more primitive ancestors."

"You mean such as the North American First Men,
those we call Amerinds? There are still many of them,
and they occupy high posts and are respected in the
Federation."

"But are they as they were, before better-armed
humans came on them and forced them to live a certain way? And is the way they live now the way they
would have grown, would have built their own culture if they'd been undiscovered?"

"No one can say," Wolfe said in Terran. "Probably
not. They would have found their own way, made their
own civilization."

"And *they* are human, of your own breed. Do you
really believe Terrans, once they won the war, would
have accepted and lived in peace with complete aliens
like us?"

Wolfe remained silent for a long time. He finally
shook his head slowly.

"When we knew of the inevitable destruction to
come," Jadera went on, "once more we used the
Overlord Stone, the Mother Lumina, to seek another
world and then to go to it."

The Lumina hanging in the air shrank and was surrounded by a lattice of shimmering crystal that looked
like pure, many-colored light, a spindle with rounded
ends. Stars came into being around it, and Wolfe realized
he was looking at a small artificial world, built solely to
house the Lumina.

"We put the Lumina in this small satellite, exactly

in the geodesic center of the Al'ar worlds, and the necessary focus was applied so our people could free themselves."

Taen shuddered.

Jadera appeared not to notice. "Then the only ones left were the Guardians . . . and this one."

"So why was I not permitted to make The Crossing?" Taen demanded.

"I do not know. There are always incongruities. If you wish, now we could use our powers and attempt to help you go with the others."

Taen's grasping organs raised, lowered, and his hood flared, subsided.

"Once, not long ago," he said, "there could have been nothing else to desire.

"But that was then. Not now. There is another task I must be prepared to undertake."

The two Al'ar looked at each other, then Jadera turned back to Wolfe. "We Guardians were to remain for a time, to make sure you Terrans could not deduce where we went, nor follow us. Then we were to make The Crossing ourselves, taking the Lumina with us.

"But then we *felt* the enemy reaching for us, *looking* for that still-existing rift into this universe.

"It is strange that not long ago we discovered a way we might have closed that rift to seal the enemy off and let him die as his universe dies . . . or let him be consumed when it is reborn. But it would have taken all the Guardians' power, plus calling on other forces, and once again using the great lens of the Mother Lumina.

"Which we cannot do."

"Why not?" Wolfe asked.

"The Overlord Stone is gone. Now we are trapped in this time, and will go in death with everything else when our enemy arrives, which will be soon."

"What happened to it?"

"Your Federation has it."

Wolfe jerked back. "No," he said. "That is false, and I do not know how your perception was arrived at."

"That is the only explanation," Jadera insisted.

"It cannot be," Wolfe insisted. "First, I was brought into this matter by a high-level Federation Intelligence official. He was—as far as I know still is—using false Lumina stones to try to find out what is going on. All he knew was that one single Al'ar might have survived, and commissioned me to find him, then later to kill him. At no time did he even mention a Mother Lumina."

"High-ranking officers do not always tell their subordinates more than what they must know. I think in Terran it is termed not letting one hand know what the other does."

"I am very aware of that," Wolfe said. "But this man, this one called Cisco, gave me all his raw data. There was no mention of the Overlord Stone anywhere in it. If the Federation had it, wouldn't they have given me different orders? And if they did have the Overlord Stone, it seems they would have insisted I take Taen alive, not kill him."

Jadera thought. "There appears to be merit in your reasoning," he said grudgingly.

"Now I shall provide a puzzler," Wolfe went on. "The Federation doesn't know about the Mother

Lumina, but the ones who call themselves Chitet do. They even know to call it the Overlord Stone."

"Who are these Chitet?"

Wolfe explained the group, their onetime attempted rebellion against the Federation, and his and Taen's murderous encounters with them.

"This," Jadera said, "is truly a puzzlement, as you said. While I consider it, I think it is time I show you why I said what I did about the Federation having stolen the Overlord Stone.

"Now it is time to show you some deaths."

* CHAPTER THIRTEEN *

Federation Hides Deadly Secret:

DEATH STALKS DREAMERS

Do the Al'ar Somehow Murder from Beyond the Grave?

By the Federation Insider's Special Investigation Team

A strange, supernatural death has struck at least a dozen of the Federation's most noted psychics and mystics, a special investigation by your Federation Insider has discovered.

According to secret police reports that were provided to your Insider's newshounds by concerned higher-ups within the government, these vision-favored men and women all died in the same manner: burning to death in awful agony. Yet none of them had time to scream or cry for help,

since in several cases loved ones or others were nearby and heard nothing.

In one horrifying case Lola Fountaine, who has frequently made predictions for your Federation Insider over the years, was in the company of her business advisor and best friend when she suddenly clawed at her throat, and her body, the terrified friend told police, showed a terrible rash, then turned red, as if burning, then the flesh charred and boiled, lifting away from the bone. "Yet," she went on, "there were no flames, and I felt no heat.

"It was almost like Lola was struck by some strange disease, some virus, that killed her by fire before she had time to call for help," the friend went on.

Lola was not the only one.

The first to die, Federation officials believe, was the late Leslie Richardson of Earth, once known as "The Great Deceiver," whose body was found on his houseboat two months ago.

With at least a dozen dead,

the Federation Insider queried officialdom as to why this horror is being kept secret. None of those we questioned had any response other than "No comment."

There are only two similarities to the deaths: All of the victims were known for their extraordinary powers; and all of them specialized in psychic investigations of the monstrous Al'ar.

Other known victims, and the circumstances of their death, are . . .

* CHAPTER FOURTEEN *

The crystal spindle's fire gleamed no more. It hung, dead, in emptiness, far from the nearest star. There were two other ships nearby. Joshua recognized them as Federation long-range scoutcraft, probably *Foley* class, built within the last five years.

"So the Federation did find the Lumina," he said. "Why was Cisco lying to me?"

"As I said previously, my explanation is that the one hand knows not what the other does," Jadera said.

"You said there were deaths here," Taen said, "so something beyond the discovery of the Lumina occurred here."

"It did," Jadera agreed. He went to another screen, touched its surface.

The image showed the Lumina carrier ship, then moved past it, into emptiness. Then there was something visible, something too small to show up on the screen.

It was the body of a human. He wore no spacesuit, and most of his head had been shot away.

"Here is the first death. None of us can tell what might have happened. One Who Fights From Shadows, bring your Terran eyes to this, so we may learn and decide what must be done next."

"Suit up," Joshua said in Terran. "We'll go visiting."

*

The entry lock of the Al'ar ship bulged outward, and three beings moved through its viscosity into space.

"Are you hearing this band?"

"I am," Wolfe said. **"You correctly set my suit's communicator."**

White mist came from the driver on Wolfe's suit, what appeared to be green light from the belts of the two Al'ar, and they moved toward the Lumina's carrier-ship.

Wolfe looked back at the Al'ar craft. Like his *Grayle*, its bulk belied the size of the crew—only ten Al'ar had been needed to man the craft before it lifted away from the Guardians' world.

The ship was named *Serex*, which translated as Swift-Strider. It was a light cruiser and looked as starkly alien as it was, with a sickle-shaped "wing" that housed the drive, fuel and weapons pods, and twin ovals that hung inside the c-curve at the front for the crew.

The cold past ran down his spine, and he remembered the war, seeing other Al'ar cruisers snap out of N-space toward him.

The Lumina's carrier-ship loomed close, and he reversed, braked briefly, and touched down on the skin of the craft. It was ridged, and he used the ridges as handholds to follow the two Al'ar to the entry lock.

Jadera touched the circle in two places and it bulged expectantly. They pushed their way through.

Wolfe looked at his suit's indicators and saw there was zero atmosphere.

The ship's interior was a single circular room, the walls lined with screens, controls. Coming down from the ceiling and up from the floor were two pylons about a foot in diameter.

The three-foot space between them was empty.

"Here is where the Lumina would have been?" Wolfe asked.

"Just so. The suspending forcefield has been shut down."

Wolfe went back to the lock and examined its edges closely.

"There are signs of damage," he said. **"Someone forced the entryway and entered who did not know the pattern of this entrance."**

"A Terran."

Wolfe nodded, then realized the gesture couldn't be seen. **"Almost certainly,"** he said. **"Would there have been any devices protecting the Lumina?"**

"None. The stone's potency is lessened by anything that blocks any sensory approach."

"So this person would have entered and seen the Lumina hanging in midair. How would it have appeared? Blank, dull, like mine, when I am not using it?"

"No," Jadera said. **"The Overlord Stone is always reflecting a measure of the energy going into the smaller stones."**

"So somebody—maybe a couple, three somebodies—boards this ship, and here's the biggest jewel they've ever seen. Real hard to figure what comes next," Wolfe mused aloud, without keying his mike. He looked around the chamber again. No thoughts, no impressions came.

"Let's go look at the other exhibits," he said.

*

The first Federation ship's outer lock yawned. Wolfe maneuvered into the small portal, saw the inner lock door was also open.

He ran his fingers along the edges of the lock, then looked at black smudges on his glove's fingertips. He unclipped a light from his belt and pulled himself into the ship's interior, the two aliens behind him.

There were nine dead men inside, grouped around the unfolded chart table. Their bodies had exploded when the lock was blown open, then, as the years passed, withered into dry mummies. Their blood and body fluids were dried red, brown, gray spatters on the bulkheads and overhead.

Wolfe glanced at the bodies, then went past them to the scout's main control panel. There was a gaping hole to one side. Wolfe touched it, again saw black on his fingertips.

He examined the controls, found the EMERGENCY OVERRIDE switch.

"Try to pull that outer door closed and turn the locking wheel as far as it will go," he asked.

Taen obeyed. **"It appears to have sealed."**

Joshua closed the override switch, saw indicators flicker feebly to life.

"There's still air in the bottles. Stand by." Again, he examined the control board, touched sensors.

Overhead lights glowed into faint yellow life.

An indicator on his suit's panel moved sluggishly. Joshua opened his faceplate.

"We have atmosphere," he said. **"Unseal your suits."**

The thin air smelled dead, dusty.

The two Al'ar slid their faceplates up.

"Why did you do this? We have no need of their atmosphere," Taen asked.

"Because it's hard as hell to do a shakedown with gauntlets. Shut up. I want to pay attention to what I'm doing."

Wolfe took his gloves off and, beginning with the first man, trying not to look at his twisted grimace, he systematically went through the pockets and pouches of the torn shipsuit. He did the same for the other nine men.

"Not a bit of ID," he said, sounding unsurprised. "Now for the ship's log."

He sat at the pilot's chair, again fingered controls.

Nothing happened.

He looked to one side, saw a small slot where something the size of a ship's log cartridge would have been. The slot was empty.

He found the ship's safe. The door had been blasted open, and papers were scattered on the deck. He knelt, went through them.

"No ship's roster, no orders, no nothing."

He went to one corpse, touched the crumpled skull, closed his eyes.

He *felt* back into dim time, *felt* surprise, horror, agony.

"Do you know what happened?" Jadera asked. **"We were unable to determine who was the murderer, since all of the Terrans died by violence."**

"Pretty sure. Let's take a look at the other ship. I'll predict we'll find one more body."

"We do not need to investigate that ship unless you

need to," Jadera said. **"It is just as you said. How did you know?"**

Joshua didn't respond but pulled his gauntlets on and turned their wrists until they clicked sealed.

*

The second scoutship showed no sign of damage, and Wolfe opened the lock and entered. There was still air in the ship. As the inner lock cycled open he wrinkled his nose, smelling what he'd expected, an echo of the familiar sweet stench of an unburied corpse.

This man had died more quickly than the others. A blaster bolt had cut him almost in two. Over the years the body had decayed slowly, the ship's conditioner system fighting against corruption: skin pulled tight against bone, ripped, tore. Fingernails, hair grew as flesh vanished. The corpse leered at Wolfe.

Wolfe went to the controls, touched sensors, and the panel came alive. He scanned it.

"Plenty of fuel . . . air . . . we'll take this one back with us."

He spun around in the chair. The two Al'ar stood on either side of the corpse, their eyeslits fixed on him.

"First," he said, **"is we get rid of *that*."**

Joshua found a thick plas tarp, rolled the remains into it, and the three lifted the tarp to the lock and cycled it out into space.

He found his lips moving in almost-forgotten phrases as the body orbited away aimlessly.

"Now, Joshua Wolfe," Jadera said in Terran. "Tell us what happened."

"It's pretty obvious," Wolfe said. "These scouts have four-man crews for most missions. Two men and one kills the other, three and it's two against one, five is cost-ineffective.

"They send them out in three-ship elements."

"Ah. There is one ship and one man missing."

"This is what I think happened," Joshua went on. "Possibly these scouts came on the Lumina craft by accident, although I find that almost impossible to believe. They've got good sensors, but space is pretty big the last time I checked.

"Maybe the Lumina ship radiated some kind of signal that could be received by someone, and they were just being curious as to the source of this signal. Or maybe they were following up on something Naval Intelligence picked up on one of the Al'ar homeworlds.

"I don't know. It doesn't matter.

"I do know that at least one member of the crew was Chitet—maybe the man that's missing, although that's not likely.

"They found the Lumina carrier ship, boarded it, saw the Lumina. The biggest goddamned jewel any man could believe. Somebody got greedy. I'd guess . . ."

Wolfe stopped, thought for a time.

"Jadera," he asked slowly, "if someone, someone who had never been trained, concentrated on the Lumina, what would he *see*? Anything at all?"

"That is almost an impossible question to answer," the Al'ar Guardian said. **"But I can hazard a thought. If someone saw the Lumina as what you said, a jewel of inestimable value, and he gazed into it, the Lumina would most likely reflect what he brought to it."**

"Dreams of glory," Wolfe said.

"This is so. I would imagine he would suddenly find his mind filled with all manner of possibilities."

"So we have," Wolfe went on, "our dreamer, whom the Lumina has just taken to the roof of the temple. So he arranges a conference on some pretext aboard one ship. One man—or woman—is left on each of the other two. Standard policy.

"Our villain arranges to be the last to arrive, waits until he knows everybody's unsuited, then blows the lock safety and the inner door open.

"He goes to this ship, kills the man here, and then, or maybe later, shoots the man on the third ship and pitches him out the lock.

"At leisure, he tries to make sure he—or she—is going to be able to disappear, and destroys all the crew IDs and the ship's log so, he hopes, nobody can know which of the twelve did it.

"Then he vacates for parts unknown, and fame and fortune, in the third ship with the Lumina."

"Why did he not use the ship's weapons to destroy the other two, and leave a completely clean trail?"

"I don't know," Wolfe said. "But I can make a pretty close guess.

"Murder doesn't come as easy as people think it does. Especially the first time out. It scrambles the brain a trifle. I remember serving a bounty once on a woman who murdered her family for the death benefits and then forged their names on bank records after it was already known they were dead.

"Our friend managed to commit eleven murders successfully. Now he's suddenly up to his bellybutton in gore. These were people who were his shipmates, maybe even his friends until a few hours ago.

"All he wants is out and away."

"I do not understand all of your words," Jadera said. **"But it appears you are making sense."**

"I do," Taen said. **"He is."**

"So our man flees with the Lumina. What would he do with it? Sell it?" Wolfe asked.

"He might think of doing that," Jadera said. **"But it would certainly take a measure of time to do. Particularly if any of the details were known in the Federation. But more likely he would, especially if he spent some time considering the stone, thinking into it, and understanding what it was** *telling* **him, realize it could be used to get him far greater riches than just selling it could ever bring."**

"What could it give an unskilled man, one untrained in using a Lumina?" Joshua asked.

"It could give him certain insights, feelings that he could follow. What someone intended, what someone was really planning, really thinking. It is likely that a man who would think of killing, who did kill, would be encouraged by the Lumina to go in evil ways. It, of course, is unconstricted by human or Al'ar customs or laws."

"So he's gone to ground somewhere and is busy trying to become the Great Nefarious Something-Or-Other. I can think of a couple of ways to go looking for him," Wolfe went on. "But first we've got to worry about the Chitet.

"I said before that I thought there was a Chitet mole—sorry for the slang, an agent—among the men and women on these ships. Some time between the discovery of the Lumina aboard the ship and the killings, he or she managed to dump a report off into N-space.

"The Chitet got that report. That's what put them in motion, looking for anything resembling a Lumina or anything like an Al'ar, since they were specifically interested in the Mother Lumina.

"Now, if they believe this is the root of all Al'ar power . . . no wonder they've been getting a little testy lately.

"Next the Federation hears about all this activity, and it's wandering around trying to figure out what the hell is going on. That's why they came to me."

"Yes," Jadera said. "That makes uncommonly logical progression. So what we must do is find out more about this scout team so we are able to track the murderer and recover our Lumina. You said you knew of some ways."

"I do. That's why we'll need this ship. It'll give me a starting point—inside the Federation. I'll start by—"

A warning shrilled in his speaker.

It came from the *Serex*.

"*Jadera . . . our sensors report transmissions coming from the ship you are aboard, being broadcast into N-space.*"

"Son of a bitch," Joshua swore. "Somebody booby-trapped this goddamned thing."

Taen and Jadera looked about, as if they would be able to see the source of the transmission.

Breathe . . . feel . . . reach out . . .

The Lumina was warm against Joshua's skin.

He *saw* the vibrations their hurried questions made in

the air, *felt* the waves the transmission from the Al'ar ship, and something else.

He pushed past the Al'ar and pulled the inner lock door open. He reached under the sill of the outer lock door and pulled out a black, soft cylinder about a foot long that had been worm-curled out of sight.

"Kill it!" he ordered, and threw it on the deck.

Taen's sidearm came out, and he touched the firing stud.

The air shattered with the blast as the bolt struck the transmitter, and the metal deck seared.

There was silence.

"Back to your ship, Jadera, Taen," Wolfe ordered. "Somebody already found these ships and set a little alarm between the time you Al'ar came here and now. Maybe they were hoping the murderer'd come back to the scent. I'll bet the bug was set by the Chitet.

"That transmitter's shouting for backup, and I'll bet it's not far away. The Chitet have everything riding on this card."

"What will you do?" Jadera asked.

"They'll want to track whoever was here. They can't know about the Guardians. You two return to the planet. I'll hang on here and give them something to chase."

"You are being foolish," Jadera said. **"We can fight them with the *Serex*."**

"They'll be coming in something big, too big for you. Goddammit, they're buying battleships! Let them chase me around for a while. If I could run rings around your watchdogs in the war, I know I can play the fox with these sobersides."

Jadera hesitated, then closed his faceplate.

"Come on, Taen," Wolfe said. "I'll get back as quickly as I can."

"No," the Al'ar said. "My life, my death, my doom are with you. I shall remain."

Wolfe started to snarl something, then stopped.

After a moment, a smile came, went.

"You have my gratitude. And it's nice to have another damned fool around. Now get unsuited and strap in as best you can. I'll try to figure out master pilot tactics in what time we've got left. Life's going to get very interesting."

Ten minutes after the *Serex* vanished into N-space, something shimmered on one of the scout ship's screens.

Joshua didn't need to key the Jane's-ID sensor.

It was the sleek, mottled darkness of a monstrous battlecruiser, only light-seconds distant.

* CHAPTER FIFTEEN *

"Those goddamned Chitet have too much money—or know too many of the right people," Wolfe swore.

"You know that ship?"

"Know of it. Class of three. Laid down during the war, never finished. It was designed to beat up most of your ships and outrun anything it couldn't kill.

"Let's see what kind of legs it's got after we give 'em something to think about."

Wolfe touched sensors and felt the scoutship lurch as two missiles fired, jumped briefly into N-space, emerged and exploded.

Two miniature suns—solar flares—blossomed.

"Now if they're blinded, they won't know just where we're going. I hope . . ."

Wolfe cut in the scout's stardrive and sent it into hyperspace.

The familiar sensations came, were gone, and the ship was in another part of the galaxy.

Joshua keyed another jump location, and as he did space blurred and the Chitet warship appeared.

"Son of a bitch! He had time to get a tracer on us! I didn't know beancounters made good E-warfare types."

Again he touched the jump sensor, and again the scout went in, out of N-space.

Wolfe swung to another panel, opened the com net, set it to scan.

"Let's see if anybody out there's talking. Maybe we can find somebody to hide behind."

There was nothing but the snarling static of the stars around them, then: "Unknown ship, Unknown ship, this is the Chitet Police Vessel *Udayana*. Please respond."

"The hell with you, sweetheart," Wolfe snarled.

"Unknown vessel, this is the *Udayana*. Be advised the pickup in your ship detected Al'ar speech. Stand by for a patch transmission."

"What is this?"

"I guess their bug was better than I thought," Wolfe said. "And now they're getting cute."

A new voice came over the com. "This is Chitet Authority Coordinator Dina Kur. I have been told there is an Al'ar aboard the vessel I am addressing. You are best advised to surrender immediately. We intend no harm, but rather a mutual sharing of knowledge."

"Yes," Taen agreed. **"I share my knowledge of everything with them, and they share their knowledge of pain-causing with me."**

Wolfe looked at the Al'ar in some astonishment. "I think you just made a joke."

"Impossible. You are deluded from the strain."

"That's twice."

"You have the word of the Chitet government," the com went on. "Here is a recorded message, intended for you, made by our Master Speaker."

Another voice came: "This is Master Speaker Matteos

Athelstan, addressing either Joshua Wolfe or a member of the Al'ar race. You have now been contacted by a high-ranking representative of our government and told that we wish to obtain certain data. We will guarantee both of you shelter from your Federation pursuers and sanctuary against any charges by the Federation.

"The Chitet are an old and honorable culture, and we wish to welcome you. Please do as the conveyor of this message instructs you."

After a pause, Kur's calm tenor came back. "That was our Master Speaker. You have five minutes to prepare to obey the commands of the vessel that is tracking you. This is the last option to avoid possible violence. Please use logic, and realize there is no benefit to be gained by further resistance."

"Jump, One Who Fights From Shadows. There is no benefit to be gained from these people."

Wolfe obeyed.

The next time they came out of N-space they saw the *Udayana*—and three other, smaller ships in a fingers formation.

Wolfe launched a missile, and two of the Chitet ships sent out countermissiles.

As he readied the controls for another jump, the *Udayana* launched. Wolfe slammed the jump button as the missile broke out of N-space and detonated.

The edge of the shockwave caught them just as they entered hyperspace, and the scoutship rocked and tumbled in reality as well as their hyperspace-altered perceptions.

"The hounds are a little close," Wolfe said. "I'm not as good a fox as I used to be."

"What direction are you moving us in?"

"Toward the Federation. We're well into it now. I hoped that they'd break off if company was around, but I'm not very lucky today." Wolfe took a deep breath. "There's another option."

"Which is?"

"I can call for help to the Federation. To Cisco."

"That would be not sane."

"Of course not. But the Chitet are going to kill us for sure. Maybe with FI we can have time to lie to them for a while."

Taen thought. **"Or, maybe, if they materialize in time, we can use the confusion to slip between the two forces."**

"Even better."

Wolfe jumped twice in rapid succession.

Now they hung in space near an occupied system—their com scanner blipped through transmission groups on several channels.

Joshua scribbled code groups from memory, then set controls on the com to the special frequency Cisco had given him and opened his mike.

"X20FM . . . DL3WW . . . DO098 . . . PLM2X . . ."

He finished the groups and punched in another jump.

"Let's get close to their sun and tart around there. Give us some time to stall."

When they came out of hyperspace, a planet was just "above" them, about the size of Wolfe's thumbnail.

"I didn't know I could shave it this near a planet," he muttered. "Taen, can you drive this thing?"

"I have been watching you," the Al'ar said. **"And I was cross-trained on older Federation vessels. I can try, as long as the Chitet do not make an attack."**

"I don't have them on any screen," Wolfe said. "Maybe we lost them. But I won't bet on it. Keep about this distance offworld, so we can jump."

He went to the chart table, opened it, and pulled out a catalog. "If I knew what I was looking for . . ."

Ten minutes later the com beeped at them.

"I could do with a little luck right now," Wolfe said, and touched the RECEIVE sensor.

The screen lit, and it was Cisco's face, disheveled, sleepy.

"Broadcasting en clair, Wolfe. We have a monitor on your frequency and he got me up. All code groups came through except one. Understood your problem.

"Suggest immediate rendezvous. Will be there on same item I was aboard last meeting to provide security. Standing by."

"Just that goddamned frigate you were pooting around in before? Come *on*, Cisco." Wolfe keyed the SEND sensor.

"Cisco, this is Wolfe. We're being chased by a battle-cruiser. I say again, a frigging battlecruiser, with three smaller friends. Same wonderful people as before if that part of the message got garbled. You better get ahold of the nearest Federation base and get some serious backup. Stand by for rendezvous point."

He returned to the catalog, thumbed pages. "Oh-ho. Maybe this."

He took a microfiche from a cabinet. Its label read: OFFWORLD WEAPONS STATIONS—TAURUS SECTOR—COORDINATES, DESCRIPTIONS. CLASSIFICATION: MOST SECRET.

"I think I have the Chitet ships onscreen now," Taen said.

Wolfe paid no attention as he slipped the microfiche into a viewer and scanned.

"Now this might do us up fine," he murmured, and went to a screen. "Just reachable. All right. Here's what we're going to do. I've got us a place to duck into until Cisco and his friends show up."

"What is it?"

"You'll see."

Wolfe went to the com and sent hastily coded coordinates through it, then replaced Taen at the controls.

"Now we go to ground. Or if they've scrapped our den out, we get killed."

Once more the scoutship shimmered into hyperspace.

* CHAPTER SIXTEEN *

The abandoned orbital fortress was a double-sided tetrahedron, Command-and-Control capsules set above and below the five weapons/living positions. The circular stations were connected by tubeways. It sat just beyond the three Federation worlds it had been built to defend, in the same orbital plane.

Wolfe and Taen stood in the scoutship's lock, waiting as the ship closed on the station. Both of them had booster packs for their suit drives.

The *Udayana* had not yet come out of hyperspace when the scout's autopilot spun the ship, and the secondary drive hissed, killing the ship's velocity.

"Four . . . three . . . two . . . let's go."

The Al'ar and human pushed away from their ship as it spun on its gyros once again and, at full drive, shot away toward the closest Federation planet.

Wolfe killed his remaining relative velocity, then aimed himself at the station. Taen was a dozen yards behind.

They were a few hundred yards from the station when the ranging radar on Wolfe's suit *bonged* and a pointer appeared on his faceplate.

The Chitet ship had just come out of hyperdrive and was closing on them. Seconds later, space distorted in three other places and the *Udayana*'s smaller escorts flashed into being.

Taen and Joshua braked, landed on the fort's outer skin, and crouched toward the nearest lock.

It was sealed.

Wolfe muttered, unclipped a blaster. He touched his helmet to Taen's. "I'll cut our way in when—if—they go right on by like they're supposed to."

The *Udayana* closed on the fortress. Wolfe found himself holding his breath.

He saw the white glare of braking jets.

"Son of a bitch," he muttered. "They *always* chase the wrong thing in the romances."

He pointed the blaster at the seal, fired briefly, wedged the lock door open, and the two slid inside.

"Did they set any wards when they closed this station down?" Taen asked.

"Damfino," Wolfe said. "If they did, we'll surely run into them, the way our luck's been running. I just hope they didn't see the gun go off."

He shone a light briefly on the lock's interior, aimed carefully and blew the inner dog away, then flattened against the lock wall.

Air howled past, subsided, and Wolfe felt the clang as still-functioning damage portals closed inside the fortress. He forced the inner lock door open, and the two went into the station.

There was an emergency repair box on the bulkhead near the lock door, and Wolfe closed the inner lock door and slid a patch over the hand-size hole he'd blown in it.

He went to the damage portal, found the entryway, and opened it.

Taen followed him, touched his helmet to Wolfe's. **"What now?"**

"Now we get out of the tin cans. I'd rather take a chance on breathing space than not be able to fight."

Silently the two unsuited.

"I assume they will be boarding us," Taen said. **"All we have to do is make their lives as miserable and short as possible until the Federation appears."**

"*If* the Federation appears," Wolfe corrected. "And if they bring something bigger than Cisco's spit-kit."

"I am looking forward to this," Taen said. **"It goes against my nature to always be running, as I have since my people left this space."**

Wolfe didn't answer, but knelt and put his hands flat on the deck.

He *felt* pain, fear, death.

He stood, looked at the Al'ar, and half smiled.

"There are worse walls to have your back against. Now let's see how badly they defanged this beauty."

*

The *Udayana*'s cargo bay was filled with men and women. They stood quietly in ranks, waiting for the commands to begin their well-planned attack.

A speaker crackled: "Seal suits."

Faceplates clicked.

"We will use the station's docking bay to debark. Make your last checks on your weaponry."

There was no need to respond.

"I have been informed," the voice said through a hundred suit speakers, "that Authority Coordinator Kur has decided to personally take charge of the prisoners when they are taken.

"This is a chance to win high status and recognition. Our enemy will use any strategy, any deception to take us, to make us allow our emotions to rule and then destroy us.

"Think well, think carefully. Fight hard, fight with the intelligence you have been trained to use."

None of the Chitet cheered as the speaker clicked off. They would have been shocked at the suggestion.

*

"Do you suppose the Federation will arrive before they kill us?"

"I don't even know if they're on the way," Wolfe said honestly.

"If so, and we are not able to slip away in the chaos their arrival will bring, have you considered what we will tell them?"

"Have you decided to allow them to capture you?" Wolfe asked, a bit surprised.

"I am not sure. But for the sake of our discussion, let us suppose I shall."

"Sure as hell we can't tell them about the Guardians, nor their planet."

"No. I specifically referred to what lies beyond, in our old space-time. What you are calling a virus."

"Do you think any of them would find truth in those words?" Wolfe said, switching to Al'ar.

"It is **a remarkable concept,"** the Al'ar said. **"Does the one you call Cisco have the mental reach for that?"**

"Again, I do not know."

"But we must try."

"Why? Why do you give a diddly damn if the virus comes through into our space? Wouldn't that be an ultimate victory for the Al'ar?" Wolfe said.

Taen looked down, ran a grasping organ through the dust that covered the sensors of the control panel in front of him, then spoke in Terran.

"No. Life is life, whether Al'ar or human. That other—that virus—is something else. And we have all agreed I am corrupted."

The deck jolted beneath them, and the slam of explosions came.

"As you said before, now it begins," Wolfe said.

"And, most likely, ends."

*

The Chitet moved into the station slowly, methodically. A squad would secure an area, take up firing positions, and a second squad would move through them to the next location.

They moved almost like professionals.

Almost.

*

Joshua's fingers rippled across the controls.

"You perform as if you are familiar with these weapons systems," Taen commented.

"Not really. I was aboard a couple of these stations during the war for a few days."

"Your movements are deceptive, then."

Three screens lit simultaneously. Joshua studied them, frowning. "Damn. They made sure this lion's toothless. No missiles, no guns, no nothin'. I guess we'll just have to take four cards and pretend there's a kicker."

He turned to another, very dim screen.

"Come closer . . . closer . . ." he said softly, hand poised over a contact.

*

A hatch slid back on the skin of the fortress, and a triple-barreled missile launcher appeared.

An alarm squawked at a weapons station aboard the *Udayana*.

"Sir," a rating said.

"I have it," the officer in charge of the position said. "Chaingun . . . target . . . fire!"

As the sailor pressed the controls, the officer snapped, "Cancel that! There's nothing in those tubes!"

It was too late.

Four hundred collapsed-uranium shells roared out the multiple muzzles of the close-range weapon and tore into the station, smashing the deactivated launcher . . .

. . . and the platoon of Chitet who were just entering that weapons compartment.

*

Sirens bellowed, echoed through the deserted tube-ways of the fortress.

"Now let us measure our foes," Joshua said in Al'ar.

Taen extended a grasping organ. Wolfe touched it, then slipped out the hatch.

*

The reserve platoons waiting in the bay shifted, murmured as the alarms threatened chaos around them.

"Silence in the ranks," an officer snapped, and the women and men were motionless.

A slender man wearing a black shipsuit appeared on a catwalk above them, lifting a heavy blaster.

He opened fire as the officer began to shout an order, and the bolts cut through the ranked Chitet.

The screams drowned out the sirens.

Return file shattered the catwalk's railing, but Wolfe was gone.

*

The squad moved slowly down the corridor. Two men flattened on each side of the door, while a third booted it open, peered inside. Their officer stood to one side.

"Nothing, sir."

"Next," the woman said calmly.

They moved to the next doorway. One man kicked at the door, and it swung inside.

He peered in, and the officer saw him convulse, drop.

He rolled as he fell, and the woman had a moment to gape at his slashed-open throat as blood fountained.

Taen came out of the compartment, slender weapon spitting flame.

*

"Sir," the officer said into his mike, "we have twenty-seven casualties . . . eleven dead. More suspected—there are units no longer in touch."

"Continue the mission," came from the *Udayana*.

"Yes, sir."

The voices were still calm, controlled.

*

There were three of them. They prided themselves, as much as a Chitet permitted himself pride, on being better soldiers than the others. After all, they had been Federation Marines before realizing the truth, deserting, and joining the ranks of those who lived logically.

They worked together smoothly, clearing passageways, reporting back to their officer on their progress.

Secretly they held him in contempt for not having the courage to stay with them, but none of them said anything.

They came to a place where several tubeways joined. They saw nothing.

They chose a new passageway, started down it.

Breathe ... fingers touching ... power focusing ... accept Zai *... become one ... become all ...*

One of them thought he heard something, looked to one side.

A blur, and then there was a man in a black shipsuit beside them. He took one step forward, leapt, and one leg shot out.

It took the first man at the angle of his jaw, and his neck snapped cleanly.

Joshua landed on his hands, rolled to one side just as the second man fired, blast searing the metal deck. Wolfe curled into a front-roll, and his legs lashed into the second man's groin.

The third's aim was blocked. She moved to one side, as Wolfe back-snapped to his feet, ducked under her swinging gun and struck twice, the first blow crushing her solar plexus, the second her throat.

The second man was trying to scream, backing away, gun forgotten.

Wolfe double-stepped forward, lunged, arm snapping forward, hips and shoulders turning. His palm smashed into the man's face, driving his septal cartilage into his brain.

Joshua watched the final body crumple slowly.

Fingers touching . . . welcome Zai *. . . let the void take you . . .*

The air shimmered, and there was no one in the corridor except the three corpses.

*

Each member of the medical team towed an antigrav stretcher behind him. They had four armed men for security, yet still moved slowly, checking every passageway.

They spun, hearing a clang, saw a duct cover from the overhead air system rolling to a halt.

One medic laughed nervously, and they turned back, and then someone shrieked.

Standing in front of them was an impossibly thin, grotesquely white being.

One Chitet lifted his gun, was shot down.

Taen pulled a grenade from his weapons belt, thumbed its detonator, and rolled it into the center of the team.

He ducked around a corner as a bolt shattered the wall next to him, heard the crash as the grenade detonated.

The Al'ar stepped back into the corridor, surveyed the dead, the bleeding, then lifted his weapon and, aiming carefully, finished the job.

*

"Sir," the officer reported. "We're still taking casualties. We don't know how many of them there are. There's one man in a black coverall . . ."

"That will be the renegade Wolfe," his superior said.

" . . . and no one knows how many Al'ar. They're all around us, sir!" His voice cracked.

The other's tones remained controlled, calm. "Very well. When one Al'ar—and Wolfe—have been captured, you have permission to kill the remainder."

"But—yes, sir." The young officer breathed deeply, reminded himself of the necessity for calm, stood. There were seventeen men and woman crouched around him, sheltering behind weapons mounts. Two hours ago, there had been thirty.

Fire . . . burn . . . take . . . all is yours . . .

"Sir," one of them said. "Look."

The officer noticed that a hose, hydraulic, he thought, had come loose from a mount. Suddenly the hose stiffened, began flailing, and a dark, acrid fluid sprayed out.

Two Chitet jumped for the hose, had it, then it slipped through their fingers, continued thrashing, the solution vaporizing as it showered them.

The officer saw a small round object coming toward him.

It seemed to move very slowly. He had all the time in the world to dive away from the grenade, shouting a warning. The grenade hit, bounced, exploded, and the fumes ignited. The ball of flame grew, devoured the Chitet, and they screamed, danced a moment in agony, died.

*

Joshua came out of the doorway fast, kicked the closest man in the side of the knee, went around him for the second.

He hit him with a hammerstrike to the temple, knew he was dead, and forgot him.

The third man's rifle was coming down from port arms. Its front sight blade caught Joshua's shipsuit, ripped it and tore his flesh.

The gun went off beside his waist, and the muzzleblast seared across his stomach.

Wolfe had the gun by the barrel, jerked, front-kicked

into the man's stomach, tossed the weapon away. The man buckled, clutching himself. Joshua doubled his fists, struck down at the base of the man's neck, let the body fall away.

The first man was flat on the deck, gagging, cuddling his knee like it was a child, trying to end the pain.

Joshua high-stepped above him, drove his heel down into the man's throat, spun away.

Breathe . . . breathe . . .

His hands came together.

Feel the earth . . . invoke chi . . .

Burn-agony seared, was recognized, denied, went away.

Wolfe ran down the corridor toward sudden shots.

*

Taen shot down the last of the five as Wolfe came in at the far end of the long room. **"They have bravery."**

"They do. For which the hell with them. Come on. I can *feel* them above, in front of us. We've got to pull back toward one of the command caps."

Taen slid another tube into the slot of his weapon and followed Joshua down the tubeway.

Let the wind take us . . .

*

The alarm gonged needlessly. The watch officer had seen what was on screen.

Three Federation battleships had come out of N-space and were, a nearby prox-detector told him, less than fifteen minutes from intercept. A gnat-swarm of other ships snapped into being around them.

The officer slapped a button and sirens howled. The *Udayana*'s watch frequency blared:

"All ships in vicinity of the Magdalene 84 Orbital

Fortress. I say again, all ships in the vicinity of the Magdalene 84 Fortress. This is the Federation Battleship *Andrea Doria*.

"You are ordered to cease all unlawful activity immediately and immediately surrender to this task force.

"Resistance will be useless. Any attempt to open fire on any Federation ship will be met with the full force of our missiles.

"I say again. Surrender immediately. Our ships will match orbits with yours and board. Do not resist!"

The *Udayana*'s commander was beside the watch officer. "Three battleships . . . a dozen destroyers . . . Mister, cut us loose from the station!"

"Sir?"

"I said seal the ship! Get us away from this station and jump into N-space! Move, mister!"

The watch officer began to say something, caught himself. He issued hasty orders.

*

The sentries in the boarding bay of the fortress had barely time to duck out of the way as the Chitet battlecruiser's lock irised shut. Seconds later, the station's outer lock closed.

They gaped and then felt the vibration as the *Udayana* broke away from the fortress into space.

One of them stammered a question, but no one had an answer.

Then their suit speakers crackled:

"Fellow Chitet. This is the captain of the *Udayana*. We have been ambushed by superior forces of the Federation. To avoid exposure and damage to our cause, it is necessary for those of you on special assignment to give up your lives for the cause.

"Under no circumstances can you allow yourselves to be captured, or to provide anything that might be damaging to the greater cause.

"You served well. Now serve on. Your sacrifice shall not be forgotten."

*

"Our rescuers appear to have arrived," Taen said.

"Yeah," Wolfe said. He saw the sniper who'd been shooting at them from behind a massive generator, and sent a bolt smashing into the man's chest. "Now let's try to stay alive long enough to be rescued.

"I hate anticlimaxes."

*

One of the Chitet ships bulleted toward the Federation units, vanished in a expanding ball of gases before it could launch a missile.

The *Udayana* and its two surviving escorts drove away from the fortress at full drive, then vanished into N-space.

The Federation admiral on the bridge of the *Andrea Doria* cursed and looked at the man in civilian clothes beside him. "We should have hit them without warning. Now we've got nobody to hang."

The Federation Intelligence executive shrugged. "They're not important. We can take them later. What's on that fortress is."

The admiral picked up the microphone, and the ancient words echoed down the corridors of the great ship:

"Land the landing force."

*

Federation soldiers spilled from the airlocks into the bays of the station.

Here, there, scattered knots of Chitet fought back. Only a handful of them disobeyed orders and tried to surrender.

The others died, as ordered.

*

"Do you know, One Who Fights From Shadows, I have a possible solution to our problem with the Federation."

Wolfe looked at Taen. The Al'ar's eyeslits were focused on him.

Suddenly Taen's head lifted, he looked beyond, then dove forward atop Joshua.

The bolt from the Chitet blaster took Taen in the back, tearing away his grasping organ and shoulder.

Wolfe heard a shout of joy as he rolled out from under the Al'ar.

Across the chamber he saw a Chitet, blaster snout aiming.

There was no thought.

There was no focus, no *Zai.*

Wolfe took Taen's death from his mind and cast it at the Chitet.

The man screamed in impossible agony, fell dead.

Wolfe did not know if he had been the only Chitet left in the compartment, nor did he care.

He knelt beside the Al'ar.

Taen's eyeslits were closed.

Joshua felt something leave, something that had been the last of a time when there was youth, no blood, no death.

His mind was still, empty.

Time passed. It may have been long, it may have been a few moments.

He *felt* a presence.

He looked up.

There were three men in the compartment. Two were Federation soldiers. They held blast rifles leveled.

The other was Cisco.

He held a wide-barreled pistol in his hand, pointed down at the deck.

Joshua got to his feet, walked forward.

Cisco lifted the gas gun, fired.

The capsule hit Wolfe in the chest, exploded.

Joshua stumbled.

He *felt* the savage insect clamor in another galaxy, building in triumph.

Then there was nothing.

SHADOW WARRIOR

Book One: The Wind After Time

Before the Great War, in a time of
friendship, the Al'ar, villainous aliens
who killed by mere sight or touch, had
given Joshua Wolfe a name: Shadow
Warrior. Now he would fulfill its
lethal promise.

SHADOW WARRIOR

Book One: The Wind After Time

by Chris Bunch

Published by Del Rey® Books.
Available in your local bookstore.

🖋 FREE DRINKS 🖋

Take the Del Rey® survey and get a free newsletter! Answer the questions below and we will send you complimentary copies of the DRINK (Del Rey® Ink) newsletter free for one year. Here's where you will find out all about upcoming books, read articles by top authors, artists, and editors, and get the inside scoop on your favorite books.

Age _____   Sex ❑ M ❑ F

Highest education level: ❑ high school ❑ college ❑ graduate degree

Annual income: ❑ $0-30,000 ❑ $30,001-60,000 ❑ over $60,000

Number of books you read per month: ❑ 0-2 ❑ 3-5 ❑ 6 or more

Preference: ❑ fantasy ❑ science fiction ❑ horror ❑ other fiction ❑ nonfiction

I buy books in hardcover: ❑ frequently ❑ sometimes ❑ rarely

I buy books at: ❑ superstores ❑ mall bookstores ❑ independent bookstores
    ❑ mail order

I read books by new authors: ❑ frequently ❑ sometimes ❑ rarely

I read comic books: ❑ frequently ❑ sometimes ❑ rarely

I watch the Sci-Fi cable TV channel: ❑ frequently ❑ sometimes ❑ rarely

I am interested in collector editions (signed by the author or illustrated):
    ❑ yes ❑ no ❑ maybe

I read Star Wars novels: ❑ frequently ❑ sometimes ❑ rarely

I read Star Trek novels: ❑ frequently ❑ sometimes ❑ rarely

I read the following newspapers and magazines:
    ❑ *Analog*   ❑ *Locus*   ❑ *Popular Science*
    ❑ *Asimov*   ❑ *Wired*   ❑ *USA Today*
    ❑ *SF Universe*   ❑ *Realms of Fantasy* ❑ *The New York Times*

Check the box if you do not want your name and address shared with qualified vendors ❑

Name _____

Address _____

City/State/Zip _____

E-mail _____

bunch/hunt heavens

PLEASE SEND TO: DEL REY®/The DRINK
201 EAST 50TH STREET NEW YORK NY 10022

DEL REY® ONLINE!

The Del Rey Internet Newsletter...

A monthly electronic publication, posted on the Internet, GEnie, CompuServe, BIX, various BBSs, and the Panix gopher (gopher.panix.com). It features hype-free descriptions of books that are new in the stores, a list of our upcoming books, special announcements, a signing/reading/convention-attendance schedule for Del Rey authors, "In Depth" essays in which professionals in the field (authors, artists, designers, sales people, etc.) talk about their jobs in science fiction, a question-and-answer section, behind-the-scenes looks at sf publishing, and more!

Internet information source!

A lot of Del Rey material is available to the Internet on our Web site and on a gopher server: all back issues and the current issue of the Del Rey Internet Newsletter, sample chapters of upcoming or current books (readable or downloadable for free), submission requirements, mail-order information, and much more. We will be adding more items of all sorts (mostly new DRINs and sample chapters) regularly. The Web site is http://www.randomhouse.com/delrey/ and the address of the gopher is gopher.panix.com

Why? We at Del Rey realize that the networks are the medium of the future. That's where you'll find us promoting our books, socializing with others in the sf field, and—most importantly—making contact and sharing information with sf readers.

Online editorial presence: Many of the Del Rey editors are online, on the Internet, GEnie, CompuServe, America Online, and Delphi. There is a Del Rey topic on GEnie and a Del Rey folder on America Online.

The official e-mail address for Del Rey Books is delrey@randomhouse.com (though it sometimes takes us a while to answer).